Other Books by Martin Myers

FICTION

The Assignment
Harper & Row, New York, 1971
Secker & Warburg Limited, London, 1971

Frigate
General Publishing, Don Mills, 1975

Izzy Manheim's Reunion
Harcourt Brace Jovanovich, New York, 1978

The Secret Viking
Martin Myers, Toronto, 2012

The NeverMind of Brian Hildebrand
Crowsnest Books, Toronto, 2018

NON-FICTION

The Urban Loft
Fitzhenry & Whiteside, Toronto, 2005

Praise for Return of The Secret Viking

"Some books make you laugh, and others make you think. It's a rare literary offering that prompts both. *Return of The Secret Viking* achieves this unlikely feat and much more. Martin Myers does it again in a novel filled with humour, insight, and a love of language. Bravo."

> – Terry Fallis, two-time winner of the
> Stephen Leacock Medal for Humour

"Reading a Martin Myers novel – the latest is *Return of The Secret Viking* – is like riding in the front seat of a rollercoaster … In the most recent instalment of his Viking series, Myers has 1,300-year-old Norseman Thorsten the Rood penning his own novel and along the way meeting up with the impediments any writer faces and wondering how to deal with them. Heaven and hell. Good and evil. Why am I here and what's it all about? … The whole experience leaves you breathless and, as with the rollercoaster, when it's over there is only one thing to do. Ride the damn thing again. Which is a good thing if we're talking about a series.

> – Jerry Amernic, author of *The Last Witness*

"Did a 1300-year-old Viking ever run a pushcart? Was he a projectionist? Did he try to hold a class reunion at which none of his fellows could recall him? And all this time was he in a coma in a well-known hospital? These are the sorts of queries that plague the reader of Marty Myers' latest piece of magical realism, a dense (yet diffuse) novel (or hallucinogenic autobiography) part of which involves an ice cream shop in Niagara-on-the-Lake (where there is no Baskin-Robbins) and a bookstore on Queen Street in Toronto (which is, indeed, on the south side of Queen Street in Toronto). *Return of The Secret Viking* also involves a wheaten terrier who writes a blog; an AI that is clearly more A than I; Tom Sawyer's Aunt Polly (who runs a b&b), and an annoying Thalia, a pink muse.

"If you think you might meet Gogol's nose, dressed as a privy counsellor, or find yourself on García Márquez' island of Macondo, or in a universe created by Salman Rushdie or Kurt Vonnegut, you'll be right at home here, in a Toronto in which a Viking (re-)encounters a millennial sorcerer.

"Maybe not. I was."

– Peter H. Salus, linguist, computer
scientist, and author in many fields

RETURN

OF THE

SECRET
VIKING

Martin
Myers

CROWSNEST BOOKS

TORONTO • CHICAGO

Crowsnest Books
www.crowsnestbooks.com

Distributed by the University of Toronto Press

Cataloguing data available from Library and Archives Canada

ISBN 9780921332961

Cover illustration and design by Xavier Comas

Printed and bound in Canada

For my family, and especially my wife Colleen, without whose help and insights this book would not have been completed.

CONTENTS

"... the entire plan of the universe consists of losing, and no matter how much we find along the way, life amounts to a reverse savings account in which we are eventually robbed of everything. Our dreams and plans and jobs and knees and backs and memories; the keys to the house, the keys to the car, the keys to the kingdom, the kingdom itself: sooner or later, all of it drifts into the Valley of Lost Things."

–Kathryn Schultz, *Lost and Found: A Memoir*

"... Then, again, maybe not."

–Martin Myers

PROLOGUE
No Ishmael, I

*No Ishmael, I. Call me author. Call me poet. Call me scriv-
ener. For I am many, many times author, poet, scrivener. But
do not mistake me for a gentle scribe or unkempt rhymester.
Know, attentive reader, that for three tumultuous centuries in
the violent Viking days of long ago, a fierce, Norse warrior poet
was I, my life and words ever in jeopardy. And now, warrior no
more, but at the core a Viking still, I persist, I endure, I am here.
Pen to paper. Fingers to keys. Tongue to cheek. Nose to the wind.
Writing. Writing. Always writing. Do you read me? Indeed, you
do. And at this very moment. And finding, one hopes, that these
words have aroused your interest.*

*I grant you that no Norseman ever spoke in this clippety-clop-
pety, pseudo-medieval manner. But it is nothing more than
a ruse, a verbal scrim, a camouflage, with which I dissemble
because my life is ever at risk. For even now, a thousand years
since the Viking epoch, were I to disclose my ageless presence
and lay bare my continued existence, risk I my life again. Should
the saga of my non-aging become public coin, who can say what
harm might befall me? I could be seized, locked up for a liar or a
lunatic. Or worse, the world could come down upon my ancient
head leaving me for dead.*

*Still, despite these fears, I find myself constrained, as I set this
down, to acknowledge the thirteen-hundredth anniversary of my*

birth this very day. Has there ever, I put it to you, been a more aged birthday celebrant? Thirteen hundred candles on the cake are not to be sneezed at. No number of sneezes would extinguish such a blaze. A tempest or tornado would it take to blow out such a vast array of flames. And a battalion of bakers to have baked the cake.

No piece of cake, however, and no small feat, to have lived thirteen centuries. Though I do not wear those centuries on my still unwrinkled brow, yet have I, by fair means or foul, doggedly slogged, century after century, through all thirteen of them, some bloody, some dreary, all worrisome. And while, on the face of it, appearing to be four and forty, forever four and forty, a good age to stay at and not to grow old beyond, I can aver, solemnly if required, that, as of this very day, have I, indeed, precisely one point three millennia of life attained. And what I have been, and what I have seen, and what I have done, and from what I have taken off and run, want surely to be set down somewhere. Well, why not here, then? When all that's done is said, is this not as good a somewhere to have said it as some other where?

Motley, motley, then, will this tome of mine be, kaleidoscopic – yes, that's the very word – assailing the mind with bits and pieces, fraught with fragments and shards, a patchwork of telling tales, a novel novel in a novel wherein I will have my say, my way and my day, as I rant away, yet alive stay, all the while revealing only inklings and sprinklings of myself, yet never truly revealing all.

Though writerly decorum demands that I maintain a certain solemnity of manner, devoid of smarm, or snotty snicker, I am, truth to tell, overcome with glee when I consider what a confounding conundrum this narrative promises to be. Tee. Hee.

Call this a hook for a book, if you must. But by this hook, or by crook, if need be, do I proceed.

From *The Secret Viking,* Book I of The Secret Viking series

PART ONE
A New Start

THE GET AWAY
Chapter 1

It was still dark on the dreary autumn morning in Niagara-on-the-Lake when Henry Wu rose early and donned the kilt he had kept tucked away in the corner of his closet. He had last worn the kilt in London, back in 1820, when he was the simple scribe and historian Walter Scott, and on that day had become the famed and beloved "*Sir* Walter Scott." That was quite a day. The thought of it almost makes him smile, but he doesn't. He's not a smiler.

Henry Wu is the latest identity assumed by Thorsten the Rood, 1300-year-old ex-Viking warrior, and smiling had never been Thorsten's strong suit, so of course, neither is it Henry's. And besides, this was no time to think about any of that. A matter of great urgency had arisen, and he is relieved to note his kilt had been spared the wrath of hungry moths during its centuries-long wait to become useful once again.

Useful? Bloody Hell! It's a godsend! Thorsten told himself. Ever since the secret of my longevity was revealed by the meddlesome Professor August Dallou, my life has started closing in on me. And now my haven and hideout, Niagara-on-the-Lake, is no longer a safe place for me to be. The area around my house is overrun with busybodies, rife with eager journalists, insistent door knockers, people milling about outside my front door trying to get a look at me, tour buses stopping to point out my house, travelers from far and wide stepping all over my flower beds, crushing my hedge, tiptoeing up my walk, peeking in my windows, wanting to talk to me, to engage me, to interview me, to get my autograph, to be photographed with me. It never stops.

To further complicate matters, the ice cream scooper from the Baskin-Robbins next to the bank has started appearing at the end of my driveway. What is he doing there? Is the scooper watching the house? What's going on? Am I under surveillance? Am I being surveilled? And if so, by whom? Is the scooper the surveillance or is he acting on someone else's behalf? Who might that someone be?

Meanwhile, inside the house, my phone rang incessantly. I stopped answering it and finally tore it off the wall.

It was only yesterday I thought that here, in Niagara-on-the-Lake, in the guise of Henry Wu, I had found the perfect hideaway, a sanctuary where I could write, enjoy my life with my wife, Mei Jun Julai, walk my dog, Presto, in the park, be as normal as I was ever likely to be. Niagara-on-the-Lake was the ideal setting for that. How quiet it had been at first, he remembered, peaceful, serene, a little gem of a place, set in a world all its own, a world of green where everything grew and flourished. That's why people moved to Niagara-on-the-Lake, including writers. It was a hideout, a secret place, a place to muse, to dream, to write, uninterrupted, unimpeded.

But alas, the inevitable has happened and once again I'm forced to run. This time my undoing is due to the fact that thanks, or rather no thanks, to that meddlesome professor of Literature at the University of Toronto, the esteemed Dr. August Dallou, who fancies himself a detective as well as an academic, and who has tracked me out, hunted me down, and revealed my long-lived existence to the world, the whole world, the *entire* whole world! Bloody Hell! And now I, in my assumed identity as Henry Wu, affable resident of Niagara-on-the Lake, as husband to Mei Jun Julai, as official companion and walker to Presto the poodle, I will have to do what I have, of necessity, done many times in my long life before, which is to say, I will have to abandon my current identity and the life I live here. If I remain, I will only become fodder for the media and be ground up in their rapacious, worldwide machine. It's time to run. Henry Wu must take off and be Henry no more.

The question in Thorsten's mind now, is "how"? How could he make a getaway with so many people watching him? And that's when he realized the answer was in his closet. That's it, my kilt, the Sir Walter Scott kilt will be my getaway costume. With Niagara-on-the-Lake being an important theater mecca, there are always strange characters in unusual garb walking around town. He himself had run into Cyrano de Bergerac on the street a few days ago. I will simply join the ranks of the players, and no one will give me a first, let alone a second, look.

And I also have that old bagpipe I bought on a whim at a garage sale a year ago. I'll use that to round out my disguise. The bagpipe was still sitting in the corner of the dining room, waiting perhaps on a haggis to pipe to the table, but since Mei Jun was not familiar with that kind of cookery, the big floppy instrument just sat there in the corner moping. And knee sox, he mustn't forget knee sox. Pipers always wear knee sox, that will pull the look together. And then he will pipe himself out of town and no one will be the wiser. He would also contrive a false orange beard. That would be easy enough, and let his hair grow out all rough and tumble. Now there's a disguise, he congratulated himself! Then I'll catch a bus to Toronto and Bob's your uncle.

And so, a few days later, Henry Wu arose while the world was still dark, donned the kilt, a clean white shirt, and the only jacket he could find, which was a black leather bomber jacket. Not perfect, but it will do, Henry thought. He taped the false orange beard to his face and mussed his hair a bit. But he had forgotten to purchase the needed knee sox, so he "borrowed" a pair of Mei Jun's which, although pink and polka-dotted, turned out to be a fairly good fit. Well, at least he was able to pull them on, that was the main thing.

Then the ex-Viking warrior, 1300-year-old Thorsten the Rood, known only recently to the gentle burghers of Niagara-on-the-Lake as Henry Wu, marched determinedly down the hallway, his kilt swinging from side to side as kilts are wont to do, and out his back door for the last time.

Why the back door? It is generally conceded that back doors are reliably better escape routes than front doors. This is especially the case when your front yard has become a Disneyland of gawkers. Thorsten could hear the coffee truck pulling into his driveway already and setting up to serve the morning crowd. Hunching down, the man in the kilt crept quietly along the hedge and then climbed the fence to the lane behind his house. He slunk silently along the back lane to the first cross street, then putting mouth to pipe and elbow to bag, jigged his way six blocks to the bus terminal.

Of all the sleepy souls in Niagara-on-the-Lake who raised their blinds to see who was making all that racket so early in the morning, not one of them asked, "Is that Henry Wu, aka the Secret Viking, running away?" Thorsten had made his getaway. He was free as a bird.

Meanwhile, back at home, Mei Jun Julai and Presto the poodle, stood together in the back doorway and listened to the sound of the pipes disappearing in the distance. "Don't worry, Presto," Mei Jun told the tousle of black curls standing at her feet. "Henry left full instructions for your walks in the park. We'll be okay." It's even possible that tears were shed, but no one knows for sure whose tears they were.

Beyond piping himself to the bus terminal, catching the bus, arriving in Toronto and making his way to the house which he had secretly rented across the street from Casa Loma, Thorsten's only plan for the future was to write and write and write, because that's what Thorsten liked to do best.

DALLOU SOUNDS OFF
Chapter 2

All of a sudden, I don't exist. Can you believe it?

My name is August Dallou. Until recently, I was a respected literary scholar and the author of numerous books on literary theory and many other literary subjects and a professor of English Literature at the University of Toronto. But now, the university won't acknowledge me in any way, saying only I'm not in their files and am unknown to them. That's not only puzzling, but also annoying. Not to mention infuriating.

You may have read about me in the first book of this series, *The Secret Viking*. I had a large and important role to play there, if I say so myself. There I was in print, in ink, on paper, in black and white. I had a house and a wife, Natalie, who cooked lasagna. I had a dog, Satch, who was not only my sidekick (my Dear Watson, my Tonto, my Sancho Panza), but who was also, sad to say, the key to my downfall. Satch inadvertently leaked the news about my discovery of the long-lived Viking, Thorsten the Rood, the most prolific writer of all time and incidentally the putative author of *The Secret Viking*, the book we all previously starred in, and therefore, it must be noted, also the author of me. But that's not the issue here.

The issue is that the reason I had so earnestly sought the Viking out and tracked him down was to bring his vast cache of knowledge to the world. And so, as he requested, I should say, demanded, I willingly promised not to reveal his whereabouts and to protect him from the notoriety he so feared. But then Satch, in a moment of forgetfulness not usual for him, pressed the wrong key on his computer (more about this later), and within mere minutes, the Viking was revealed to the whole world.

The result was that the Viking, in a pique of anger declared me non-existent. "There is no Professor Dallou," he told the world. "There never was. I made him up. That's what writers do. We create characters and that's what Professor August Dallou was. He was a character in a book I wrote." And with those words, Thorsten summarily wrote me off. All my work and efforts were denied. 1300-year-old Vikings really know how to get even. They've had lots of practice.

So where does that leave me now? Well, for starters, I'm here. That must mean something. The problem is that if I'm here, but I don't exist, I'm no further ahead. Non-existence is a bit of a downer, don't you think? That's certainly the case when you have no job and no place to live. Now I'm in the trash heap like a beaten-up old book, spine broken, pages torn, falling apart, collecting dust on someone's shelf or in someone's memory, trying to look interesting on a shabby table in a secondhand bookstore. Suddenly, I'm nobody to anybody. And all because my author said so. But wait. Me, a nobody?

Well, here's the real news. Maybe he, my know-it-all author, is the nobody here! Right from the start, he was an impossibility. I, at least, was possible, even plausible. I, at least, had believability on my side, as well as my academic credentials, and the legion of students who thronged my lectures and shared their ideas with me. The elements of my existence are, and always were, in plain sight. If I don't exist, as the author claims, it has never exactly hindered me or my activities in any way.

But talk about convoluted, and it's about to get even more so. The long-lived Viking may actually be the author of himself as well as of me. Now, that doesn't happen every day. So, as I mentioned earlier, maybe he's the nobody, the one who doesn't exist. There are people who believe that, but not me. Remember, I'm the one who chased him around the world and back, tracked him down, interviewed him, recorded his stories. He even made me cry once, but I don't want to talk about that.

It's clear to me he exists, and he's out there somewhere, and I need to find him to straighten out the mess he's left me in. Or to get even, if I can't. And if that sounds too severe, consider what he's done to me. Here I am, no job, no place to live, declared non-existent, and stuck in limbo. This being of no fixed address is no fun, I can tell you and so can my wife, Natalie, and our dog Satch. I need to find that shifty Viking, but he has disappeared again. If he's operating true to form, he will by now already have a new name and a new place to hide out, and I don't know where to begin looking for him. The conundrum in all of this is that not knowing where he is or who he is now makes him not only unfindable but also unrecognizable if found, and thus hard to ferret out. That's an overly long sentence but it conveys the complexity and the frustration of the search I am about to engage in.

In addition, the author who claims to be writing this book, or novel, or whatever he's calling it, the book you are reading here: he should know who the Viking is purporting to be right now and where to find him. But if he does, he's not sharing that information. Maybe he's keeping it for a future "reveal" in this story. Or, his creation may be hiding from him, and the illustrious author doesn't have the foggiest idea where his creation has gotten to. Or, even more upsetting, his unlikely creation, the 1300-year-old Viking, may not, as others have claimed, exist. The fellow I'm searching for may be nothing but a figment. So, here's what I'm faced with: I need to find the Viking and get my situation sorted out, but if the Viking doesn't exist, if he's a figment, how do you find a figment? Figments are hard to find. That's why so few of us look for figments, at least the people I know.

The problem is further complicated because what if the author who purports to have written what you are reading now doesn't exist either? True, his name may be somewhere on the book you're holding, the cover, the spine, the title page, but that doesn't mean a thing. Any one of us could have put it there. And I, as the narrator, as you may remember, I, too, don't exist. I'm only a hired hand doing this on behalf of the author but what does that mean when the author doesn't exist? Who am I working for? Why am I doing this?

The long and short of it is that it's not easy being non-existent. People tend to put you down and dismiss you when they find out you do not exist. They can be insufferably righteous. My advice is never trust the righteous. They are cheats, liars and hypocrites. And sometimes, other distasteful things as well. They believe it's a dog-eat-dog world, which is bad enough since it's a cliché, but what makes it even worse is that in a dog-eat-dog world where the dogs don't exist, you don't know what you're eating. And if you persist, you're looking at malnutrition or a shortage of dogs.

I'm married to a scientist named Natalie. Natalie doesn't exist. She is the granddaughter of a famous scientist who used to exist but no longer exists. Natalie and I have no children. So, they don't exist either, but for different reasons. You can't deny that there is a certain logic to this.

Our dog, Satchimotomonkeyman, is a wheaten terrier. We call him Satch. It saves time and he doesn't mind. Satch doesn't exist. And doesn't speak. He can't. Nonetheless, he has taught himself to read and write and contributes a weekly column called The Dog Log to the *Post*. It was in his column he inadvertently spilled the secret of the reclusive Viking's whereabouts, sending the reclusive Viking into a towering rage. The result of it all was that Natalie and I, along with the canine perpetrator of the exposé, were evicted from our house to an as yet undisclosed venue leaving us in a kind of limbo which we hoped was temporary. But who knows? So far, we are definitely nowhere. Maybe he is punishing us. Authors can be flaky.

Later, after we were summarily evicted from our house, neighbors interviewed by a nosy reporter told him they had never ever laid eyes on me or my wife but thought, perhaps, that they might have seen our dog although they didn't know his name, which is not surprising since he doesn't exist and they didn't get the *Post* where they would have seen his column, and read his byline. It's hard to know where we're going with this since the non-existent have the freedom to go anywhere they please, do anything they please. So, there is at least one good thing to say about non-existence, and that is that there is no greater flexibility than the state of not existing. If you doubt this, ask any non-existent person to confirm it and they will.

If my author will not expeditiously extricate Natalie and me from our limbo, and I suspect he will not, the heartless lout, I have a couple of options for my future. One is consulting. My area of expertise is literature and all things literary. It's possible the world may be ready for a non-existing literary consultant. My other option is to find another non-existent author who is understanding of my current predicament and persuade him to write me into his latest book as the antagonist. I've had a lot of experience with antagonism and do it well.

Natalie, ever the practical one, feels that with my sterling credentials, I should not be restricting my opportunities by talking only to non-existent authors and should instead be talking to best-selling authors who exist. And in fact, I have taken this to heart, and I am now having discussions with Stephen King and Neil Gaiman about my prospects as an antagonist. It will be difficult if I have to choose between them. If both turn me down, there is always Margaret Atwood who has found me amusing.

One more final thing. Satchimotomonkeyman, our beloved Satch, has confirmed that no matter what we do next, he is with us 100% or more, if required. He's not good with math.

If I sound peeved, that's putting it mildly. But I'm no Iago acting out for no reason. I'm no Dostoevsky, "Without god anything is possible." I'm Paddy Chayefsky, "mad as hell and I'm not going to take it anymore." I will find the Viking, I will take back my life, my wife, my job, my dog (who else can I talk to and let the reader know my mind? besides I love the pooch). I will take my cues from my creator of old, that elusive fly-by-night, disappearing act of a Viking. I will dance like a butterfly, waft like the wind, I will sneak around, hide in the bushes, spy from the treetops, I'll hang over him like a storm cloud and rain on his parade. I will wipe him off the map, that heartless, run-away, deserter, no-show Viking, write him out of the book, and let the world see that I do so exist. I'm here and I'm mad.

THE HELL OF CHAPTER ONE
Chapter 3

Blinking and squinting at the glare of his computer screen, Thorsten sits hunched over his keyboard, hands poised, yet hesitant, trying to plot at least a tentative route, if not the actual plot, through his new novel.

Now that I think of it, Thorsten tells himself, Samuel Taylor Coleridge was never one of my identities. I never claimed to be, never pretended to be, never wanted to be, good old Sam. No slight intended to his RIME OF THE ANCIENT MARINER, for which I have nothing but the greatest respect, but only recently did it dawn on me that I, Thorsten the Rood, by virtue of time and tide and good winds, was, and still am, the original, ancient mariner.

And now, hanging heavily around my neck, I have my own albatross. Here I sit before a state-of-the-art computer in an ergonomic chair in a splendid house across the street from Casa Loma in the good and bustling city of Toronto, but there is no wind in my sails. The stream on which my mind drifts may seem safe but under the surface, rocks and rapids lurk.

Between books now, the already written Volume One on the one hand and the not yet written Volume Two on the other, I find myself in a worrisome place, pressed and stressed and flanked by the two tellings. Wrestling with memory and fencing with logic, the two books seem to lean in menacingly.

Even for the most skilled of scriveners, setting down that first chapter can be hell. But despite the popularity and overuse of the expression, all hell doesn't break loose. When you're a writer, and your particular brand of hell closes in on you, it doesn't roar around on your desktop, real or virtual, spilling your ink or performing a war dance on your keyboard. Instead, it rages around in your head, thwarting your efforts.

The challenge of Chapter One is to somehow seize readers from word one and entrap them into submission, ideally breathless and excited submission. This involves capturing them in the telling before they lose interest, give up, and run for the exits.

There has to be some simple, yet suspenseful way of starting a novel. I've done it before, not without success in Book One. Subscribers to my blog said the opening chapter of that book had seized them by the throat, filled their minds with apprehension, left them breathless with trepidation and, yes, they averred, though the suspense was, at times, almost unbearable, they couldn't stop reading.

A number also said they couldn't wait for the next book, but I'm having trouble getting started. This will not do. I simply can't let readers down. They're counting on me. And I'm counting on them. Without readers, where am I? Nowhere. That's where. In the shallows and stuck on the rocks.

I've been thinking that, in my dual role as author as well as protagonist, perhaps the smartest thing for me to do is to try to reconcile with Professor August Dallou, the antagonist and foil in Book One, whom, I admit, I unfairly ousted. Now, after much consideration, it seems to me that I should write him back into

Book Two as scholar-turned-sleuth once again. I have to confess that with that obsessive detective mindset of his, he could often be a bloody nuisance. At the same time, I have to concede, he could also be very helpful. I have of late come to appreciate that he was hardworking, extremely knowledgeable and second to none in all things literary. And his persistence was nothing short of remarkable. Truth to tell, he kept me on my toes and there wouldn't have been a book without him.

But the thing is, he repeatedly pissed me off, so I wrote him out of the book and denied his existence. I understand why he's so angry with me. To be honest, I handled it badly in a moment of overblown annoyance. Obviously, if I want him back in this book, I will have to reconcile with him, reassure him of my respect for his many talents and come up with a suitable residence for him and his wife, Natalie, and for Satch, that amazing, remarkable, well-intentioned but not always reliable, dog of theirs.

I think what I'll do is call a former character of mine, Aunt Polly, and arrange for August and company to stay in her Bed and Breakfast for the time being, while Professor Dallou and I try to sort things out between us.

THE MUMBAI PAPERS
Chapter 4

The moment he turned the corner he was struck by the multicolored package sitting in his office doorway. Even from a distance it was a bedraggled presence, definitely not one of those neat, brown, oh-so-rectangular boxes from Amazon like those sitting in everybody else's doorway.

It has to be a mistake, he thought as he climbed the stairs and examined the beaten-up, stickered-up package leaning against his door. Written all over with many colors of smudged ink and pasted up with enough stamps to fill a collector's scrapbook, it may have been a sorry looking mess, but it wasn't a mistake. It bore his name, and his address:

> Cary Harnett, Publisher
> Horizon Books
> 1232 Laurel Crescent
> Toronto, ON
> 6X5 L9Z
> Canada

There was, however, something odd about it. As well as his current address, the package also bore every address he had lived in for the past ten years. He could see traces of his previous abodes written in a rainbow of colored inks and then crossed out or partly pasted over with newer addresses until finally it got to the right address. If all that wasn't puzzling enough, the package was mailed from Mumbai, of all places. Who did he know in Mumbai? Nobody, said Cary to himself. Absolutely nobody.

Upon opening the package, he discovered what he had already guessed. The package contained a manuscript, the kind of manuscript he often got from young authors hoping to find publication for their first novels, not realizing the process of getting published was more complicated than simply shipping your bright and shining new novel or collection of stories off to a publisher and crossing your fingers that this cherished work would find it's convoluted way out into the world and onto a bookseller's bookshelf. Cary, at this point, would have done as he had done many times before. Ordinarily, he would have packed the parcel back up and marked it "Return to Sender." He hesitated this time not only because the return address was unreadable, but also because he wondered who, in far-away Mumbai, might even know about Horizon, his small publishing company. And adding to the mystery, there was no accompanying letter of explanation, only a yellow sticky note that read, "When we taught at Hopkins, you reacted positively to some of my stories. I thought you might like these as well. I have no plans for them. I am currently writing screenplays for Indian films." The note wasn't signed, but there was no question in Cary's mind that the note was written by Seth Whittle! Seth Whittle! My gawd! Seth Whittle, his long-lost colleague and confidante of many years ago. He couldn't believe it! Both he and Whittle had been teachers and writers at Johns Hopkins University in Baltimore, Maryland, and had quaffed many a pint at The Jolly John Barth, a popular on-campus bar, comparing teaching notes and sharing their own literary struggles, metafictionally, of course. We had much in common, Cary remembered. I was a huge fan of his writing. But after my term was up and I left Hopkins, Whittle also moved on and I lost track of him. No one seemed to know where he had gone or what had become of him. The Hopkins records were no help. The university was as puzzled as I was. Or more so. Seth Whittle, it appeared, had dropped out of the scene, off the map, and out the door.

But now, after all those years, here he was back. But back where? Mumbai? Well, perhaps. There was another enclosure in the package, a faded newspaper clipping from the Mumbai Mirror announcing the formation of a new film production company, Stirring Films, led by someone called Stuart Ogden. But who the heck was Stuart Ogden? And what did he have to do with Seth Whittle?

And there was another thing about the package that troubled Cary. That little yellow sticky-note. What was he to make of that little yellow sticky-note? Cary found it disappointingly cryptic. It made him wonder if he was being toyed with. There was no way to know, no way to find out, and with no legible return address on the package, there was no way to locate the sender. He was sure the package had come from Whittle, the stories certainly appeared to be in his style, but it was odd, he thought, that Whittle hadn't signed the note or added a personal message. That would have been nice, after so long. And he didn't know what to make of the newspaper clipping or the name Stuart Ogden.

The fact was he didn't know what to make of any of it, so he immediately sent a letter off to Stuart Ogden at Stirring Films. Then waited. And waited. But even after several weeks, there was no response. Another letter went out. No response. A check with Google revealed Stirring Films had ceased making films a few months earlier.

Cary briefly considered publishing the stories, but other commitments intervened, and the papers sat in their much-battered box on the corner of his desk, and over time faded from his attention and from his intentions. Then, about five years ago, the media suddenly went ape over the discovery by a University of Toronto English professor of a 1300-year-old Viking, Thorsten the Rood, who had stopped aging at 44 and was still secretly living in our midst. The secret Viking, having moved on from warrior to author over his many long years of life, had hidden himself behind a series of writers' identities, and one of those contemporary identities, Cary was startled to learn, was his former friend and colleague, Seth Whittle. Startled doesn't really cover it. He was dumbfounded.

He immediately tried to contact Whittle, or Thorsten as he was now revealed to be, through the Viking's professorial discoverer at the University of Toronto, August Dallou, but with no success. Neither responded to messages nor acknowledged Cary in any way. He would have persisted, but then, a short time after all the media fuss, the newly discovered secret Viking disappeared again, vanished into thin air, and had not been seen or heard from since. Nor, curiously, had the academic who uncovered the Viking's existence. The university said only that he was not in their employ.

In the course of all this commotion and excitement, Cary learned that the secret Viking had written a book called, not too surprisingly, The Secret Viking, purporting to be about himself and including some of his stories. Overcome with curiosity, Cary bought the book and read it to try to learn more about this unlikely, long-lived, mega-writer. Reading this work convinced him that the stories he now calls "The Mumbai Papers" were almost certainly written by the secret Viking whom he had once known as Seth Whittle.

If you haven't already read it, The Secret Viking recounts the backstory of what you are reading here. In the event that you are unfamiliar with the novel, here is a brief, 256-word synopsis of that tale: If you are already familiar with it, feel free to skip the next two paragraphs.

Researching deceased novelist Helga Rittersporn, literary scholar August Dallou discovers she had been working on an exposé of her Polish novelist husband, Myroj Krupinski, who had abandoned her a few years before her death. Dallou is taken aback to discover that Myroj Krupinski was an assumed identity of a 1300-year-old Viking warrior-poet, Thorsten the Rood, who had stopped aging after a blow to his head at 44. Aware that despite not aging, he was mortal, and could expire from illness, accident or violence, Thorsten has had to learn to live peacefully, unobtrusively, obsessively guarding his secret to stay alive.

And so, as the warrior ebbed, the poet flowed, practicing his writing craft all over the world, frequently changing place and name and wives and families. And now, 1256 years later and still hiding behind a series of cover-up identities, mostly literary, the life–extended Viking walks in shadowy secret among us today. Recognizing Thorsten as possibly the most prolific writer of all time and a trove of literature and history, Professor Dallou turns detective, determined to find the elusive warrior-poet and persuade him to share his thirteen centuries of knowledge. As Dallou chases Thorsten through numerous current identities, the secret Viking's tale spools out in glimpses of his protracted life, his writings, past and present, fragments of his work as poet, scribe, novelist, playwright, interspersed between episodes of Dallou's persistent hunt. In the end, Viking author and learned scholar collide in a surprising conclusion which, vaulting from book to book, is transfigured here into a surprising continuum.

Paragraph skippers start again here:

In any case, here am I, Cary Harnett, small press publisher in Toronto, Canada, with a stack of unpublished work by a once-upon-a-time Mumbai screenplay writer, who was at one time my best friend, and now is, or was, or pretends to be, the long-lived Viking, Thorsten the Rood, and I've finally decided to publish those stories.

THE CALLING
Chapter 5

"You have called an encrypted number. To speak further, you will need a password."

"I don't have a password. "

"Did you receive a message on blue notepaper?"

"Yes."

"Are you holding the notepaper?"

"I am."

"Does it have a watermark?"

"Not that I am aware of."

"Please, hold it up to the light. Now, do you see a watermark?"

"Yes, I do."

"Can you make out what it says on the watermark?"

"It's a number."

"Six digits?"

"That's correct."

"Can you read the number to me?"

"It's 648753."

"That is your password."

"You've never asked for a password before."

"We're expanding our reach and require more security."

"Fine. Why have you contacted me this time?"

"I have work for you."

"Okay, I'm listening."

"This is an assignment with three possible stages. Stage one will involve your locating of a target person, a male in his forties."

"Understood."

"When he has been located, we plan to negotiate with this person. But if negotiations fail, the assignment will require you to go to the second stage, which will be to engage in a physical abduction."

"Which is to say, a kidnapping?"

"Correct. You know the drill."

"Yes."

"The final stage, if all else fails, will require the use of your full hardware package."

"The full hardware package. Uh huh. Well, that will cost you."

"I'm aware of that."

"Good. How do I locate the target?"

"We don't know where our man is at the moment. He's a

master of disappearance and disguise and has so far eluded us.
However, we have learned that a colleague of his, a Professor
August Dallou, will shortly be moving into a Bed and Breakfast
in Toronto where he will be waiting to meet the target. You will
observe Dallou and inform me when he makes contact with the
target person."

"Got it."

"We have not discussed your fee."

"If the assignment goes full length, my fee is one million US
dollars."

THE OPENING STRETCH
Chapter 6

Aunt Polly was no stranger to dudes of all stripes. It was clear to her that the unsmiling, somber dude, in his black designer suit and Wall Street tie, standing on her doorstep with nothing but a backpack in tow, was not exactly your average, free-range, grass-fed cowboy. The first thing she noticed as she craned her neck upward to see his face, was that her visitor was at least seven feet tall. He appeared to have arrived in the black, chauffeur-driven limousine parked in front of the sign that announced *Aunt Polly's Bed and Breakfast.* And there was something else, something she tried not to make too much of, and that was the cold look in his purplish-blue eyes. It seemed to her that when he looked at her, he also looked right through her, simultaneously accepting and dismissing her with his gaze, his cold, piercing gaze. His name was Sidney Wilks, he told her, but he answered to Stretch, which he much preferred.

He had shown up that morning unannounced, looking for a place to stay. Did Aunt Polly have a place for a new lodger? Yes, she did. But she was taken aback when it became clear that the tall guy was not looking for standard accommodation. His puzzling and implausible intention was to rent a shower enclosure.

A shower enclosure? Aunt Polly, though amused by this odd request but not fazed by it, was agreeable until the would-be shower enclosure renter revealed he was planning to sleep in the shower. The shower, Aunt Polly then disclosed, in all good conscience, had a slight leak which would not only drip on the shower's inhabitant and make him soggy at the very least, and sopping at the very worst, while he was trying to sleep, but was likely to keep him awake as well. This, she was able to convince him, was less than an ideal sleeping arrangement. But she had another suggestion, a compromise plan to which, after some discussion, Stretch agreed.

He would make do with a closet instead, and Aunt Polly emptied out one of the closets and he moved into it, shut the door and apparently slept soundly in it, held upright, in a slightly crouched position, in the cramped space, looped in by his Walmart purchased, Dominican crafted, rubber mesh suspenders clamped onto the waistband of his pajama bottoms at one end and hung over a brass coat hook on the closet wall at the other.

The next morning while Stretch silently picked away at the breakfast Aunt Polly had prepared, she watched him carefully, but could not shake her initial reaction to the tall stranger and the strangeness in those cold, purple eyes. If she expected Stretch to tell her more about himself, she was wasting her time. Nor was there an explanation for Stretch's oddball sleeping arrangements. He kept that to himself too. His reticence to communicate was not budget driven as Aunt Polly had originally assumed. In fact, it soon became clear, money was no problem for Stretch. He was surprisingly solvent. He had a bank account and several high limit credit cards, and he paid his rent in advance with earnings from his practice which he described as "consulting." His work could take him away for a few days two or three times a month, he explained cryptically to Aunt Polly, mostly to other cities, occasionally to other countries.

"Who is this weirdo?" worried Aunt Polly. It worried her all morning and all afternoon and well into the evening until, unable to resist her concern, she went online to search the archive of Stretch's hometown newspaper, the Mount Airy News. What she found there increased her concern. Apparently, while he was serving in Afghanistan, Stretch had been singled out for clandestine, special operations. Right from the get-go he had proven to be a sharpshooter of uncanny accuracy. He had the top scores not merely in his company, but in his brigade, which led to a series of significant sniper postings and numerous marksmanship medals which he never spoke of or wore. Settled into a sniper's protective crouch, he single handedly pursued his precarious military specialty with precision and deadly purpose, wiping out strategic installations and human targets, where he was a highly specialized, cold-blooded killer. The article went on to praise his military skills to such a degree that Aunt Polly was sorry she had gone snooping. What she learned only increased her original misgivings about her new, secretive and very disturbing boarder.

And when the next day, early in the morning as she was just starting to prepare breakfast, the black limousine pulled up in front of the house again and the unsmiling driver opened the back door for her new resident to get in, Aunt Polly knew. She knew without the shadow of a doubt. She knew unquestionably. She knew, no ifs ands or buts about it, that there was no way on earth that this much celebrated shooter could be a consultant, as he had termed himself. What she didn't know was how, or why, or what he was up to. She just knew it was all bad news. And there was no one she could discuss this with.

And then, the phone rang.

"Hey, Aunt Polly."

"Hey, yourself."

"It's Thorsten."

"Thorsten! To what do I owe the pleasure of your call, old friend? Are you going to come and stay with us?"

"Afraid not. Not at the moment. But I'm going to send an interesting couple and their dog to stay with you for a while."

"Okay. When are they coming?"

"I'll have them there later today, if that works for you."

"It works. Do they have names?"

"August and Natalie Dallou, and their dog, Satch. August is an English professor, Natalie's a scientist and Satch is a wheaten terrier. August is a former colleague of mine and it looks like we may be working together again soon. In the meantime, they need a place to stay till they get settled."

"I'll treat them gently and feed them well."

Aunt Polly breathed a sigh of relief. The spinning in her head slowed down, ground slowly to a halt. This Professor Dallou, a *bona fide* scholar, was about to stay at her B&B. He was learned, knowledgeable. A professor! He would make a learned assessment of the danger, the ruthlessness, of the man called Stretch.

Professor Dallou would be able to sort out whether Stretch was just a tall tale or the real thing, the deadly, dangerous, maybe even heavily armed, real thing.

The doorbell rang.

"Coming," said Aunt Polly.

In the distance, a dog barked.

THE DOG LOG BLOG
Chapter 7

Hi, everyone. Satch here. I'm back finally with an online news-letter, The *Dog Log Blog*. I hope you missed me; I missed you. Sorry, I've been unable to write my last few *Dog Log* columns because we were displaced for a while, and I lost my job at the *Post* and couldn't get my paws on a computer that I need to write with. You may recall – if you don't, let me remind you – that I taught myself to write when I was a puppy, but a keyboard was the only way I could manage it. I tried pens and pencils and even a stylus, but I just couldn't get my head or my paws around any of them. I even briefly considered dictating my column to a recording device, but I lacked the physical speaking appara-tus to do it with. As you may gather, gear can only go so far and often that's not far enough. It should be no surprise that I can't talk, and when I barked, growled, whined, or whimpered, all I got was unreadable, unspeakable, wall to wall (actually, edge to edge) jumbles of illegible type.

That's why I got very excited when I discovered that Aunt Polly, with whom we're staying temporarily, at her Bed and Break-fast, after being summarily evacuated from our house of long standing without explanation, had a laptop. It's odd, since learn-ing how to write, the laptop has been my device of choice. I've discovered things about myself that I'd never even thought of before. The more you know, the less you know.

But let me get back to the explanation I referred to above. Because August and Natalie Dallou, my beloved owners, and I, were evicted, abruptly, you might say, from our previous residence which had been created for us by the secret Viking who, it appears, had a sudden change of heart because he was furious that his secret had leaked out, albeit, inadvertently in *The Dog Log* due to my carelessness for which I'm very embarrassed. It must have pissed him off big time because abruptly, with no notice or explanation, we didn't have a place to be or to stay. The world's most mysterious author had written us off, written us out of existence, out of the house, and out onto the street. Although we hoped for equivalent replacement accommodation, it hasn't happened yet, doesn't appear to be happening and we're very concerned that it may not happen. We're not sure where we stand, or why, but at least we know where we sleep since, as noted, we're staying in a Bed and Breakfast for the moment, Aunt Polly's Warm & Friendly Bed and Breakfast. I don't know what we'd do without Aunt Polly. Actually, I do know but I can't bear to think about it or write about it.

Nonetheless, I'm worried that the differences between August and the secret Viking, the bad blood, if I may put it that way, could escalate further, and August is getting increasingly rancorous about it, spouting angry declarations and uncomfortably colorful curses, promising to get even with the Viking whom he blames for our displacement and our being pushed into non-existence.

It's no fun being a dog when your master is angry most of the time and you're not sure if you exist or not. Something has to be done. I'm not sure what it is but I'm working on it. If you can bear it, bear with me.

I apologize for jokes, if you find any. I also apologize, if you don't find any.

And above all, I apologize for barking at you.

Woof!

PAPER TRAIL
Chapter 8

No one had to tell him that his long, intense and lonely preoccupation with writing could, would and did, sporadically deteriorate into a dreary dead-end. He knew only too well that it could, would and did. For whatever reason, or for no reason whatsoever, there were times when just getting the bloody words down on the page could be depressingly difficult. During those dismal times, he would despair of being able to continue writing, and this was one of those times.

But it hadn't always been this way. Once, after several fallow months of agonizing introspection and recriminatory self-appraisal, a sudden surge of creative energy had propelled him into a relentless burst of productivity. Night and day, for three weeks, he had written almost non-stop. And because he loved the printed word with a passion and was eager to hold in his hands the writing he had wrought, he was constantly printing out what he had been frenetically keying into his computer. The green signal light on the printer blinked reassuringly and the faithful machine hummed sonorously as it delivered sheet after sheet after sheet of his precious words into his eager hands and the waiting world. Whenever he took his eyes from the monitor, he would contemplate with rising elation the rising pile of paper that his efforts were producing.

Writing and rewriting, printing and reprinting constantly, he drove his laser printer on through vast forests of 96 white, twenty-pound, multi-purpose, xerographic paper, which he ordered online on the internet and had delivered to his door at regular intervals, ten reams – 5000 sheets – at a time. The paper arrived in ten packages of 500 sheets each, in a sturdy corrugated carton bound with strong nylon strapping. As per his usual practice, he would cut the strapping, open the carton, unwrap one of the packages and load his printer, which had two paper trays holding 200 sheets each.

One day, as he was about to load the second tray, he noticed that one of the sheets was not blank. It had been written on. Puzzled by this, he read what was on the sheet. To his surprise, it was a penciled note, which said:

Can somebody please help me? I'm trapped in a paper factory. I don't know how I got here. But I'm all alone and I can't get out. There's not another person in the place. It's totally automated, cranking out sheet after sheet, ream after ream, of paper, packing it in packages, putting the packages into cartons, sealing the cartons with strapping and transporting them on moving belts to somewhere in the building that I can't see or get to, but that I assume must be a loading area, where the cartons are picked up by trucks and then delivered.

I've been putting this message into a lot of packages, in hopes that it will be found by someone who will help me escape. The windows are barred. The doors are locked from the outside. I can't get out. My cellphone battery has died. There are no phones here. I can't call out. I might as well be in jail. I'm a virtual prisoner here. I'm living on chocolate bars and twinkies out of a vending machine, but the stuff is stale and I'm running out of change. If anyone gets this message, please, please, I beg you, call 911 and tell them to come and rescue me. I don't know where this place is but a poster on the wall shows the internet address as Acme Papers.

Oh god. Will someone please help!

Gareth Brink.

Thorsten remembered contemplating the message at length; he thought it might be a prank. Or maybe a ploy to drive buyers of printer paper to the company's website. He found the message hard to believe. It didn't feel real, somehow. It could be a hoax. Still, he thought, what if it were the real thing and this poor devil really was trapped? He couldn't just leave him there, could he? He telephoned 911 and told them about the note he had found in his printer paper package.

"We've had over a hundred calls this month from people who've found the same note in their printer paper," said the operator who took the call. "But here's the odd thing. We haven't been able to find Acme Papers on the net or off. It doesn't appear to exist."

"Are you saying the message is a hoax?"

"We're not sure. We're still looking into it. The name on the note is the same as that fellow who disappeared in his car on the QEW a while back. He phoned us for help, too, but we couldn't find him. The investigation team feels that this may be a copy-cat thing, probably written by a professional writer as a prank. Don't be surprised if it turns up on YouTube or in a book some-day soon."

"Well, I'm sorry to have troubled you. I've wasted your time with this foolishness."

"No trouble. Better safe than sorry. That's what we're here for."

As he hung up, something that he should have thought of earlier struck him. Acme Papers was the paper supplier from which he had ordered his paper supplies on the internet. Yet, according to the emergency operator, they hadn't been able to track the company down. How could that be? He went to the internet and typed in the address, the one he had always used, and got back the message: 'The specified server could not be found.' It made no sense. He had just taken delivery of paper from them. Now, he would have to order paper from someone else, if he could figure out who that someone else would be. Would it, he wondered, also come with a note in it asking for help?

This is what happens, the esteemed, hard-working author told himself, when a character from Book One of a series stubbornly refuses to get out of the author's way and insists instead on continuing with his own story in Book Two. Fiction, it seems, can get in the way of real life. Or maybe it is real life.

LORDY
Chapter 9

Out of the clear blue sky, down like a thunderbolt, came a thought into that battered head of his. Where, oh where, is Gee Oh Dee? he wanted to know. Hey, Gee Oh Dee!! Where the heaven are you? Pray, talk to me, Gee Oh Dee. I have a question."

Not receiving a reply, he tore off into a rant, which could at any time accelerate into a full-blown harangue. I know you must be thinking may god in his infinite mercy spare us from a hectoring harangue.

The question is, whose infinitely merciful god are we calling up? Yours? Theirs? Everybody's? That's a lot of gods, right up there with Old Norse mythology, which was overrun by gods, for heaven's sake. But with so many gods out there, or up there, or in there, or over there, in whose god are we supposed to believe? Whose god are we to trust? Whose god are we to worship and adore? Whose god is the right one? How could there be a right several?

The questions keep coming quick and fast. How about truth? Let's talk about truth. For some, god is the ultimate truth. But despite all we've learned, after millions of years on earth, a universally agreed upon truth about our existence continues to dog us, to outfox us. For the faithful, truth has been replaced by faith which has been defined as unquestioning belief, or belief for which there is no proof. The faithful argue that since truth itself is temporary, fleeting, and open to question, it, too, can never be proven. The faithless don't quarrel with that but argue in rebuttal that faith should also be treated as temporary and shifting and open to question.

What's worrisome is that at the extremes of faith, at the bleeding edge, so to speak, of almost all persuasions, the intolerably intolerant, the rigidly, frigidly devout have always clung unwaveringly to their own particular and unshakeable version of faith, from which they will not be dissuaded. Instead, they go about their business resolutely dragging their old baggage with them wherever they go, never for a moment stopping to open it up and question what's inside.

Why does a lapsed Viking like me get so incensed about all this? Why do I work myself into an ironically evangelical fervor over Gee Oh Dee? It is, after all, just babble, as in the tower of, preserved, enshrined, ennobled, meaninglessness, made to appear to matter by its being faithfully and reverently written and re-written and meaninglessly mumbled and re-mumbled. This unrelenting, unenlightened, unquestioned reiteration has led, amongst the willing and more easily deluded, to what was deemed to be a dialogue – albeit a one-sided one and hence an oxymoron – with one or more – depending on affiliation – invisible, supposedly superior beings who, alas, never show up, never answer the phone, never retrieve messages, never call back, never leave word or voice mail. Never!

LORDY, LORDY
Chapter 10

"We have to talk," said Thorsten to the presently sleeping, allegedly superior being. Somehow, it sounded mighty like a prayer, but how could it be? He never prayed.

"Why do we have to talk while I'm trying to sleep?" responded the allegedly superior being, through his sleepy torpor.

"Because I haven't been able to get through to you while you were awake, if you ever are. Lord knows, I've tried."

"Maybe you didn't try hard enough."

"Come on. That's a pretty lame argument coming from god the creator."

"You think being god is easy? Well, I have news for you. The stress is almost unbearable. I'm entitled to a little rest now and then, you know. You have no idea how much I have on my plate."

"Oh yes, I do. As author and thus god of this fractious fiction, I am only too aware of the burdens of godship. And just between us gods, I'm also aware that you, sir, don't exist in reality."

"That's pretty funny, coming from you. Need I remind you, cantankerous sir, you don't exist in reality either."

"Correct! That's precisely the point. For purposes of this discussion, we're on equal footing, just two non-existing gods debating each other's non-existence. You can't beat that. How symmetrical. How precedent setting. How revolutionary."

"That's all very well, angels on the head of a pin. But this discussion is eating into my sleep time. So, let's get on with it. What do you want to discuss?"

"I want to discuss your inaction, your absence when help is needed, your disdain for the flock you are supposed to shepherd."

"All right. But first let's talk about your ungenerous attitude toward me and my loyal adherents. I'm god, after all. You could show a little respect. Or even political correctness. I'd settle for that. I want to know why you constantly deny me, constantly naysay me, constantly question and berate those who believe in me? Why do you keep pissing on my parade?"

"It's not a parade. Santa Claus has a parade. You don't have a parade. And I'm not pissing. If I were, it would be on your sandals. What's more, I don't think you've read the news today."

"News?"

LORDY, LORDY, LORDY
Chapter 11

On Wednesday, October 9, 2008, just after 9:00 p.m. EDT, people of all faiths the world over were shaken to suddenly learn that the god that had always been there for them, more or less, was there no more. God, the creator of old, was gone. Bye, bye. How could this possibly have happened?

The concept of God the Almighty had shuddered to a sudden and sobering end when astronomers and astrophysicists at The Deep Space Institute in Waterloo, Ontario, excitedly announced that they had discovered extraterrestrial life. This, they hastened to add, was not mere speculation. They had been able to confirm, in two-way communication, that the extraterrestrials existed, were a highly advanced life form, living, not as one might have expected, on another planet, but in a pleat, or a wrinkle, or a fold, or a seam, or perhaps even on a cuff, or a lapel, somewhere in the fabric of Space/Time.

Fortunately, these extraterrestrials, these advanced beings – it was hard to know what to call them – were not warriors. They were scientists and appeared to be peaceful and unthreatening. That was the good news. The not so good news was that these cosmic explorers were engaged in research on a galactic scale, and had, in fact, far, far, and even farther, in the distant past, created life on earth from basic molecular building blocks. They had been bemusedly monitoring the evolving results for eons –

in earth time – through all its ups and down, its flips and flops. For them, the planet Earth was a space laboratory in which they observed humans on Earth in the same way earthlings study ants in a glass box ant farm.

It devastated god's people on Earth to learn that the god they thought was there for them wasn't and, it now appeared, had never been. This alarming information was greeted by the faithful with shock, quickly followed by consternation and disbelief. The doubters among the believers were many and quick to dismiss this scientific turn of events as science fiction. The names of earth's various and sundry gods were invoked angrily, pleadingly, but in vain. God, the Creator, was nowhere to be found. The god that used to be, the god that formerly was – was no more. There was a new guy in town.

Howdy!

INFO MONSTER
Chapter 12

The cheery atmosphere at Aunt Polly's had not infiltrated August Dallou's smarting sense of injury. Still angry and dispirited at being written out and off by Thorsten, and sitting at Aunt Polly's kitchen table, brooding over a cup of recently brewed but no longer hot coffee, August Dallou cudgeled his brain trying to decide what to do next.

That bloody Thorsten. He sticks us in a boarding house and disappears. Where the hell is he and how do I find him?

Casting about for something either methodological or, if necessary, magical, to ignite his imagination, Dallou opened Aunt Polly's computer and was set aback by an ad that immediately popped up on the screen. It was an ad for Giggle, the most prodigious and prestigious of the search world's giants. Giggle was, the ad informed him, a search engine light years ahead of the competition, light years ahead of its time. This past-the-postmodern marvel, this irresistible, irrepressible, renowned and redoubtable colossus was a towering trove of data, a fount of knowledge, a high rise pile of possibilities like no other trove, fount or pile, a virtual vessel purported to contain all the knowledge, all the wisdom, mankind and womankind and any other kind of kind you might care to include that had been accumulated, and maybe, even some that had not yet been accumulated but were pending thanks to Giggle's aggressive, forward looking, stop-at-nothing algorithms. The ad went on, extolling the new campus at Ontario Place which was now open to direct contact by searchers.

That's it! How fortuitous! The excited Dallou leapt from his chair. I'll present myself in person at the giant search engine's headquarters, and finally get some answers.

And so, it was decided. He would make a personal appearance, live and redundantly in person at the gates, as it were, of the tower of knowledge. He would arise and go there and be there and stand there before the prodigious giant and confront and consult the almighty research colossus face to face. And surely it will know where Thorsten the bloody Rood is now!

Ideally located on a man-made island afloat in an inlet in Ontario Place, Giggle provided complementary parking, VIP appointments, and all-day childcare, as well as an all-you-can-eat buffet restaurant that offered, in daily rotation, the cuisines of worldwide cultures. It was not only eminently convenient but also easily accessible. This enabled Dallou, although he had no children in his care to worry about and was no fan of buffet restaurants, not only to appear in person before the giant search complex but also to have what was, in effect, an audience with the high-tech phenomenon that was almost religious in its glory and grandiosity. It, somehow, came across like a high-tech place of worship making him feel that the god he did not believe in, nor in any way acknowledge, was on his side because... well, you never know.

What more could he ask of a search engine? Well, just about everything, as it unsatisfactorily transpired. His visit should have been a slam dunk, but it turned out to be just a slam. And not just one slam, but one slam after another, a series of slams. The mammoth search engine, the brilliant behemoth, the most advanced, most capable, most comprehensive internet service provider on the whole overheated, overpopulated, overburdened planet was either glitch-ridden or infected with an erratic sense of humor that it playfully toggled on and off at its wayward algorithmic whim.

He had begun bravely, clicking decisively on the button that said 'Start Here,' whereupon there immediately appeared a gigantic giggling mouth with the word Giggle, all upper case and bold, between the lips instead of teeth, filling all 300 cubits of the giant computer screen followed by a great clicking and clacking and buzzing and bleating, and trumpets blaring and trombones blaring back, and flower petals in a multitude of hues, shapes and sizes floating down from on high as an empty search box popped onto the screen in which to enter the subject of his search. And abruptly faced with this empty space awaiting a response, Dallou realized with a jolt that he had absolutely no idea what to enter.

He had no current identity of his quarry to offer, no name, no location, nothing. All he had was the mystery he was chasing and the unanswerable question: How on earth was he supposed to identify the subject of his search when he had no idea of who the Viking was now or what he might be calling himself?

He tried typing in the Viking's original name: "Thorsten the Rood."

Giggle Response: "Error. Check spelling."

"1300-year-old Viking."

Giggle Response: "Invalid entry."

"Warrior poet."

Giggle Response: "Oxymoron."

At his wit's end, Dallou decided to try the most recent identity that Thorsten had hidden behind: "Henry Wu."

This time there was a palpable pause before Giggle's Response: "Which one?"

"Which one? What do you mean?"

Giggle Response: "There are 1400 Henry Wus in Hong Kong alone.

"Try Henry Wu in Niagara-on-the-Lake, Ontario."

But this time, Giggle offered no response to Dallou's request. Instead, there was a long pause and Dallou was beginning to fear the interview had come to a halt. Then, all of a sudden, the machine blasted out a tone so low and rumbling that it shook the 300-cubit screen as well as the ground that Dallou stood on. The blast was followed by a pop-up accompanied by sirens. The pop-up read: Updates available. Restart computer.

But the machine offered no instructions to activate a restart, and after several failed attempts by Dallou, followed by several more blasts and several more restart messages, a notification popped up on the screen that read: If you do not know how to restart the computer, you can ask Althea to restart it for you.

Before Dallou could worry about how exactly he was to ask this

"Althea", whomever, whatever, wherever she was, to restart the computer for him, a robotic voice spoke.

"Hi. I'm Althea. How can I help you? You can tell me after the tone."

This was followed by the sound of a tone best described as an algorithm in agony, an algorithm on its knees, an algorithm in its last throes.

"Althea, restart the computer for me."

"Don't you mean, *please* restart the computer for me?"

"Althea, please restart the computer for me."

"Please enter your username."

"AugieD."

"That does not match the username we have on file."

"What username do you have on file?"

"Not AugieD."

"That can't be. That's the username the phone company gave me."

"That would explain the problem. Phone companies are notorious for errors. Let's try your password. Please, enter your password."

"Malfeasancetype2."

"Repeat password."

"Malfeasancetype2."

"There appears to be some uncertainty."

"Are you certain?"

"This is a tentative response. It's difficult to be certain about uncertainty."

"Does that mean you won't be able to restart the computer for me?"

"More data required. "

"What data?"

"Are you sure you are who you say you are?"

"Not anymore."

"Security question: Please enter first name of the person you are looking for."

"I don't know what it is at the moment. It changes."

"That is not a correct answer."

"Is it possible that this is not a good day for questions?"

"All things are possible."

"Are there better days?"

"Sometimes. It varies."

"Maybe I'll come back and try you on a better day."

"While you're here, you should try the Giggle All-You-Can-Eat Buffet." Althea sounded more friendly now. Almost human.

"'I'm not…"

"They're doing Albanian today."

"Albanian? I had no idea they had a cuisine."

"Everybody has a cuisine. Mother Theresa was Albanian."

"Did she ever have the All-You-Can-Eat Buffet?"

"I don't think so. She wasn't much of an eater. But you could try it."

"Maybe next time."

"Please, repeat your reply."

"Maybe next time."

"Do you have any other responses you wish to add?"

"Maybe next time."

SMOOTH SAILING
Chapter 13

In the meantime, the object and subject of Dallou's Giggle search, the Viking, was taking a break from the novel he was trying to write. Perhaps, his mind would benefit from a review of his early days and Viking ways.

During the 300-year Viking era, or the Viking heyday, if you prefer, being a Viking was all about sailing. But no Viking ever claimed that it was smooth sailing. I certainly didn't. Mind you, smooth sailing has a certain smartass ring to it. Smartass just like most of us were.

Let's be serious. As a *bona fide* ancient Viking, albeit out of context, out of costume, in deep disguise and full makeup, I can certify with a high degree of certainty that if, way back when, a Viking had said it was smooth sailing, he was playing word games. These days, of course, everybody is playing word games and not only word games. Games, all manner of games, are huge right now. Playing games or gaming, if you prefer, is the hot, new lifestyle. Gamers abound. What else are gamers to do? If you're an ardent gamer, feel free to abound.

Based on my own centuries long, personal, often painful experience and the jokes I used to make about it, I can tell you however that Viking for a living was not a game. The singular, unrelenting fact of the Viking era was that you couldn't let your guard down even for a split second. If you made that mistake, you could be wiped from the face of the earth with the swipe of a sword, or the snap of a longbow. Then, again, you could be hacked into parts one and two with just a single whack of a broadaxe. You had to stay alert. Being a Viking was many things, but it was not a game.

Nonetheless, way back in yesteryear, many of us rebellious, young males, at odds with our would-be-farmer fathers who, having grown weary of life at sea, were trying to exchange sea-going for crop-growing, while their stubborn, male progeny persisted as stir-the-pot hot-heads spoiling for a fight. What a rotten lot of shifty shit disturbers we young were, I confess, in guilty retrospect, plain and simple.

We were restless. We were reckless. We were feckless. Even in the early days, when at every opportunity, we would tear off in all directions in those sleek longships of ours and go wreak havoc somewhere, no matter where, as long as it was elsewhere, so we could raid and run, raze, burn, pillage and scoot back to our ships laden with loot and quickly sail home.

History records, and old Norse literature confirms, that among this trouble-prone, bad-news bunch of louts, there existed a cadre, that I like to think of as lusty but lofty, arts-prone lads, troubadours, mostly, minstrels, warrior poets, if you will, I, among them. Given were we, this loud singing, word slinging crew, to declarations and perorations and dissertations and rolling phrases and rhythms and rhymes and extended poems that ran for miles on good days.

But sometimes, they only ran a few feet and then just sat, short and squat, begging to be egged on and cackled over.

THE GIGGLE WRIGGLE
Chapter 14

Put off by Giggle but as stubbornly determined as ever and in no way defeated by the puzzlingly erratic and peculiarly unhelpful behavior of the oversized search engine, August Dallou decided not to give up but to engage with the giant facility again and hope to have better luck on the second time around. What kind of game were they playing? He'd see if he could figure it out.

Dallou's second visit to Giggle started off promisingly enough, when, as he approached the search engine from the parking lot at Ontario Place, Althea, the automated voice, greeted him cordially even before he could address the colossus or tap any of its buttons.

"Hey, AugieD," said Althea. "Welcome back."

"Thank you," said a surprised AugieD.

"Long time no see," said Althea.

Actually, it had only been a couple of days. What was she talking about?

"How've you been, AugieD?" persisted Althea.

"Fine. I'm fine."

"You here for the buffet?"

"The buffet?"

68

"The Giggle All-You-Can-Eat Buffet"

"No. I…"

"It's Thursday. We're doing Lithuanian today."

"Lithuanian? I'm not familiar with Lithuanian cuisine."

"Oh, they don't think of it as cuisine. They just call it Maistas which is food. No familiarity required for Maistas. Familiarize by eating. All you can eat. Today we're featuring eight of Lithuania's signature favorites: Cepelinai, Kepta Duona, Burokėlių Sriuba, Kibinai, Saltibarsciai, Grybukai, Kugelis and Raguolis. All you can eat! $19.95. Go for it. Comprehensive tasting notes accompany each classic Lithuanian dish."

"Tasting notes? Like they do for wines?"

"Same idea. Read before you feed. Be sure you read the notes, AugieD."

"I'm not here to make choices or read notes! I'm here to make a search!"

"I see. You're searching for a Lithuanian this time? Is that it?

"No. Not a Lithuanian. I'm looking for a Viking."

"But it's Thursday."

"What does that have to do with it?"

"Thursday, we do Lithuanian."

"What day do you do Viking? "

"There's no day for Viking in the current rotation. Maybe in the next rotation. I'd have to check with scheduling. Would you settle for a Lithuanian in the meantime?"

"I'm not a settler. I'm a searcher. I'm searching for someone specific and he's not Lithuanian."

"How specific?"

"Can you find the secret Viking for me?"

"The secret Viking? Why didn't you say that in the first place?"

"I didn't know there was a first place."

"There's always a first place. It's an inflexible, mathematical certainty. There's no getting around it. Which one is in first place for you today, AugieD? *The Secret Viking* book or the secret Viking person? We have both."

"The person, absolutely."

"All right. How about the secret Viking as Franz Kafka?"

"Do you have somebody more recent?"

"How about Miguel de Cervantes?"

"I think you'll find that's less recent."

"Oops! Sorry about that. Any of these talk to you? Christopher Marlowe, Herman Melville, Aesop, Geoffrey Chaucer, Joseph Furtado, we recommend Furtado, a little known but nevertheless impor…"

"Stop! I'm looking for the Viking's current identity. Who is he now?"

"That would be the person calling himself Henry Wu at the moment. He had been living in Niagara-on-the-Lake with a female companion, who may be someone else."

"Someone else? Who might that be?"

"Unfortunately, that is not known at this time. "

"It doesn't matter. I'm not looking for her. What about him? Where is he?"

"He appears to be…" Althea hesitated before continuing, "to be on route to somewhere."

"To somewhere? That's a little vague. Do you have a destination?"

"Not yet. It may be pending."

"Pending is no help. Is that all you can tell me?"

"For now. Sorry about that. Our algorithms are only human."

"In my opinion, algorithms are not human."

"Like humans, they are not without flaw or glitch. Maybe more will be known when whoever he is gets to wherever he's going, whenever that is or will be."

"But you don't know whomever he is, or whenever he will get somewhere, or wherever the somewhere will be when he gets there. Good god, Althea, he must have bought a ticket to somewhere."

"It is difficult to be specific when there is unresolved destination vacillation. Whatever Mr. Wu's destination may be it may not be his final journey's end. Or he may not be there yet, still in transit. He may be held up in an airport, between planes. Or he may not be travelling by plane. He may be on a train. Or on a ship. Or on a motorcycle. Or he may be walking. Or, in fact, he may be going elsewhere. Many of those we search for often decide to go elsewhere after they leave and before they arrive where they were originally going. It's difficult to keep track of plan changers."

Here, Althea paused before continuing. Then, with honey in her voice, she added, "Would you, by any chance, AugieD, know where Mr. Wu is going?"

"Me? You're asking me? No, absolutely not! I have no idea where he's going. That's what I'm here to find out!" Dallou shakes his head in disbelief. "I would have to say that this is very perplexing."

"It is," interrupted the digital voice that didn't sound very digital anymore. "That's why so many clients change plans and go directly to the Giggle All-You-Can-Eat Buffet. It's much simpler to get to, no travel involved, not to mention more filling. You could follow their example and go there too."

"I don't want to go to your All-You-Can-Eat buffet. I've already eaten. It is urgent that I find the specific person that I came here to look for. That would be the secret Viking aka Henry Wu. Can you help me, or not?"

"Not today, I'm afraid. You could try us again tomorrow. We may know more. Tomorrow is Friday. On Friday, for the Giggle All-You-Can-Eat Buffet, we're doing Ethiopian. No cutlery. You eat with the injera. Do you know about injera?"

"No, I don't. And I don't want to know."

"It's made with…"

"I don't care what it's made with."

Once again, Althea was talking in circles. Something was not right. For whatever reason, she was stalling, evasive, pitching the buffet again. And did Althea really think he would know where Thorsten was going? None of this made any sense.

But here was the real puzzle: was it possible that Giggle was also looking for Thorsten? Now, there was a worrisome thought. His mind harkened back to how the ad for Giggle had popped up on Aunt Polly's computer the instant he had turned the machine on. It was as if it was there, waiting on him. Dallou was suddenly overcome by the outrageous thought that he was somehow being dragged into a plot, that none of this was an accident. Could it be that the research colossus was trying to trick him into serving up whatever information he might have about Thorsten?

Luckily for Thorsten, thought Dallou, I don't know anything about where he is at the moment. They'll get no information from me. But what's going on here? I don't like the sound of this.

WHEREFORE GIGGLE?
Chapter 15

Why would anyone call such a prodigious, top ranked, globally praised, search engine Giggle? The name was always a strange choice. For one thing, the name Giggle makes light of impressive technology. For another, it comes off as fanciful and perhaps even frivolous. In other words, it treats the concept of the super-sized search engine as a sort of gargantuan amusement park. How helpful is that?

The fact is that Giggle was not the search engine's original name. The giant computer was invented in Belarus, of all unlikely places, the brainchild of a sixteen-year-old computer nerd named Casimir Smirkovsky while he was still a Minsk high school student. He came up with the idea following a severe concussion suffered when unwisely playing football without a helmet and being knocked for a loop and blacked out for six weeks. After recovering consciousness, Smirkovsky worked determinedly on his rehabilitation for six months in the National Library of Belarus, speed reading the enormous collection of Belarusian printed material, said to be the largest in the world, as well as the third largest collection of Russian language books in Russia.

Eidetic imagery, a result of the scrambling or unscrambling of Casimir's mind by the concussion, enabled him to rapidly access, retain and recite almost everything he laid eyes on. Amid this lengthy and demanding exercise, the giant search engine concept that simplified sorting and cataloguing all the acquired data in his head presented itself to him in a kind of daydream. It won him an instant global following and transformed him at eighteen into a billionaire, and the youngest oligarch in the Russian Federation. But like every success story there was a dark side in which fingers were pointed, hatchets were honed, and careers were demolished.

Taking the darkness of the dark side as a signal of things to come that would require precautionary measures, Casimir quickly de-Russified and decamped to Switzerland, managing his burgeoning global network from Zeebach, a country town outside Zurich where he lived, and continues to live, anonymously, known only to his personal Swiss banker who has never been publicly identified, except by number. Based on the precocious inventor's truncated surname, the search engine that made his success originally was called Smirk. When, after it attracted worldwide attention, a translator noted that 'smirk' in English was rather unfriendly and even pejorative, Casimir decided the name should be changed to something a little more positive but not uncomfortably earnest. Giggle was the choice of a jury of English-speaking consultants. But electing to maintain a minor but respectful connection with the inventor, the jury decided not to abandon Smirk. Instead, it was demoted to a sort of subtitle attached only by a diminutive colon and for a time the search giant was known as Giggle:Smirk. Before long, this unprepossessing arrangement wearied of the maladroit linkage and 'smirk' digitally deleted itself off the page, so to speak, except for its password protected presence on a file tab in the computer of Casimir's anonymous Swiss banker.

As you may recall and as August Dallou soon discovered, one can find out almost everything one needs to know on Giggle except when the devious digital behemoth decides, for reasons of its own, to be recalcitrant and not cooperate. Having become suspicious of this erratic behavior, Dallou wondered if perhaps the reasons were not its own.

Which led to the questions: Whose reasons were they? And what were those reasons?

A WALK IN THE PARK
Chapter 16

The old, pine kitchen table at Aunt Polly's had lots of room under it for Satch to hang out waiting for treats from the tabletop to be passed to him, in case he lost interest in the bowl of Canine All-Star Kibble that Aunt Polly had set out.

August, engulfed as he was in his own sense of precariousness and still furious with the Viking, did his grumbly best not to be surly but was not entirely successful. From under the table, not surprisingly, Satch said nothing but couldn't help thinking, "Wouldn't it be nice if Augie and Thorsten got their acts together and made up? But how can they make up if Augie can't find the Viking?" He wished there was some way he could help. There wasn't.

During the scrambled eggs, August Dallou's cellphone rang. He stopped eating. Who was calling him? Eggs on fork, on-hold in mid-air, he seemed to be trying to decide what to do. Natalie decided for him.

"Augie. Answer your phone."

"Right," said Augie, wolfing down the scrambled eggs while the phone rang again.

"Answer it, Augie."

Reaching for his phone, August wondered again who the hell

could be calling so early? Who even knew he was still around? "Hello," he answered gruffly.

"What took you so long to answer?" said the phone.

"I was in the middle of a hearty breakfast which your call so callously interrupted. Who is this?"

"August. It's me," said a familiar voice.

Pause.

"Thorsten? I don't believe it."

"I don't either."

Dallou took a big breath. "What do you want?"

"We have to talk."

"We are talking."

"I mean face to face. I know you're angry, August, but let's not have a shouting match on the phone. Let's meet and talk."

"Where?"

"I'm just across the street in Bellwoods Park. Come over."

" Where exactly will I find you?"

"I'll be sitting on a bench under the giant oak near the Gorevale entrance."

The caller hung up his phone and Dallou shook his head in disbelief.

"Natalie, you're not going to believe this! The world's greatest disappearing act has just reappeared!"

"There are times I don't believe any of this." Natalie was ever wise.

"He must want something. What further abuse does he intend to inflict upon us, I wonder?"

Even as he waited for the traffic light to change before he could cross Queen Street West, Dallou could see, just as described, a park bench under a giant oak that was said to be 800 years old. The light turned green. Dallou marched briskly across the street, walked towards the bench and stood directly in front of it looking about for Thorsten, but the bench was empty, and Thorsten was nowhere to be seen.

"What the hell is going on?" He looked up and down the street, scanned the park, but there was no Thorsten. "He's done it again. I should have known," muttered the annoyed Dallou. "I can't believe I just fell for another one of his tricks." He turned on his heel and started to storm off. "What could he be up to this time? That blasted Viking."

The grass grew green and tall in Bellwoods Park, and the park gardeners were out in full force that morning in their noisy vehicles. One of the lawn trimmers in a red ball cap, a blaring Hawaiian shirt, reflective shades and mischievously sporting an orange goatee that looked decidedly phony, climbed down from his machine, and bearing a cardboard tray with two cups on it, walked toward the bench under the old oak.

"August! "he shouted. "Come back. I brought us coffee."

Dallou stopped mid-stride and turned around.

"Thorsten? Is that you?"

"Of course, it's me. Who did you expect? Donald Duck?"

"Well, I didn't expect to see you all Hawaiianized like this. Are you going to a luau or something?"

"I'm just trying to stay anonymous. C'mon, let's sit."

But Dallou, ignoring the invitation to sit, stood facing his adversary.

"Why did you call? What do you want to talk about? Because I've got a few things I'd like to talk about too."

"Relax, August. Relax. Let's just chat."

"Fine. Let's chat. What are you doing here in Toronto?"

"Writing a bit. Fiction. My latest novel just won the Booker."

"The Booker? I had no idea."

"You're not keeping up, August."

"Actually, I am keeping up, dammit! I've managed to maintain all my literary interests and activities. In fact, I watched the Booker on TV, but I didn't recognize you. Pretty good disguise."

"Thank you. I've had some practice."

"Now, looking at you in this setting, two titles come to mind, *Waiting for Godot* and *Sparring with Socrates*."

"Look, August. Let's be clear. You do not write the titles. You do not write the chapters. You are not the writer. I am the writer.

I write the titles. I write the chapters. You are a character in my book. You are a professor, a sometime detective, and a complete pain in the ass. And right now, you do the listening till we sort this out. So come on, sit down, drink your coffee, a fine dark blend, by the way, called Midnight from the Black Cat Roastery across the street, best in the neighborhood, and listen up. I'll be Socratic, and then you can have your turn."

Dallou sat and took the cup of coffee Thorsten offered, "Okay, I'm listening, but spare me the condescension."

"No condescension intended. Truly." Thorsten took a deep breath and continued in a friendlier tone. "August, you know better than anyone, chasing you down like this is a first for me. I've never sought out anybody this way before. Ever. August, I called you. Weren't you surprised?"

"Of course, I was surprised. And I'm wondering why."

"Because…" Here the orange-goateed Viking in the screaming Hawaiian shirt looked down, groping for the right words. "Well… I missed…" Then he continued with more determination, "I missed our meetings, that's what I missed. I missed our long talks together, August!"

There was no reply from his bench partner, so Thorsten shuffled his shoes around in the grass and gravel under the bench, and finally, after a lot of hem and haw, blurted out, "Damn it, August, It's YOU. I missed YOU! There. I've said it. I missed YOU. That's why I called."

Dallou was speechless.

The Hukilau shirt continued, "Back then, back in Book One,

we were a pretty good team, weren't we, August? You and I? …
and we were…" groping for the right word again, "…not just
colleagues, we were… we were… *friends*… right?"

"Friends? Hah! You had a strange way of showing it, Thorsten."

"Oh, c'mon, August. I know you're furious with me about how
I treated you, but understand, I had to put my foot down. Need
I remind you of what you did to me? You and that smartass dog
of yours wiped out 1300 years of secrecy with one click of the
computer. Suddenly, I was thrown to the media like meat to a
lion. And you expect me not to be incensed?"

"Now, just a minute. Look what you did to me. You declared
me non-existent! You took away my house, my job, and then
you told the world I didn't exist, never had existed! You… you
dumped me, that's what you did! You really know how to get
even, Thorsten!"

"Yes, well, I guess I overreacted. I was upset! I panicked and lost
it. I'm sorry. I really did behave badly. But you have to admit
that you had done me an extremely damaging disservice."

"All right. All right. But you know as well as I do that it was an
accident. No harm to you was ever intended by either Satch or
me. So, now, can I tell you my side of this?"

"Not yet. There's one more thing. Since we're clearing the air,
let me add that I was very hurt by your publicly threatening
me… *I'll follow him like a storm cloud, rain on his parade…*
that whole infantile tirade. You were a bit over the top, don't you
think? Admit it."

It was Dallou's turn to grope for words and shuffle his feet.

"Okay, you're right. That makes two of us, I guess. We were both over the top. We traded tantrums. I'm sorry, Thorsten."

A light breeze rustled the oak leaves. The man sporting the orange goatee stood up. "Look across the street, August. See that bookstore?"

"Type Books. Good name for a bookstore. What about it?"

"There's a poster in the window. What does it say?"

"Coming Soon. *Return of The Secret Viking*. Hey! That's you!"

"I'm writing a new book, August."

"You're forever writing a new book."

"Wait a minute. Don't be so patronizing! I'm not a book writing machine, you know. It doesn't come easily. It's a lot of hard work. And that's my problem. I'm trying to start a new book but I'm kind of stuck. That's why I called you."

"What exactly do you want from me? How can I help?"

"I want you to come back, to be part of the book, to play the role you used to play so well. I want you to move the plot forward, to liven up my story, to kick my ass, to point out my flaws and misdemeanors. I want you to keep me honest, to keep me open-minded. I need you as backup and backstory and backstop. In short, I need you back and in my new book. Okay? What do you say?"

"Hmm. Well, that's a long list. I'm flattered, but, well, I may have other offers pending."

"Don't be ridiculous, August. Kiss them all goodbye and let's get to work. I can count on you, right?"

Dallou turned serious. "Before we go any further, Thorsten, there's something critically important I have to tell you."

"Aha! You see, I was right. You're starting to work already!"

"This is serious. Just listen to me. Here's what's been going on. I've been trying for a week now to locate you through Giggle. I wanted to sort out the situation you left me in, and I thought Giggle might help me find you."

"And did it?"

"No, obviously. I didn't find you, did I? You found me. Just hear me out. I think there's something strange, very strange, going on with Giggle. Something worrisome. Something you should know about."

"Spit it out, August. What are you talking about?"

"In my session with Giggle, it became clear that the blasted, know-it-all search engine knew a lot about your past."

"Well, of course I don't like that. I don't like it at all. But I guess that's what search engines do. They know things."

"But Thorsten, it knew you too well. It knew your past identities, almost to a person, as far as I could tell. Were you ever really Franz Kafka?"

"Actually, I think I was. But, dammit, August, what are you talking about? Nobody knows all my past identities! I can't remember half of them myself!"

"Well, Giggle knew them. Knew them in detail. Starting way back in history and right down to Henry Wu and your time in Niagara-on-the-Lake."

"Bloody hell!"

"And it also knew that you were on the run from Niagara-on-the-Lake."

"Well, I guess that's no surprise. It was all over the newspapers. But did Giggle know I'm here in Toronto?"

"No, I don't think so, and that's where my interview turned really strange. Althea, the digital spokesperson said you were "in transit," but she wouldn't or couldn't, I don't know which, tell me where you were in transit to. She waffled. And then, get this Thorsten, she tried to pump me for information about you. Can you believe it? The search engine started searching me! She wanted to know if I knew where you were! "

"Bloody hell."

"And there's another thing." continued Dallou. "During my interview, Althea persisted in changing the subject repeatedly, babbling on about various cuisines and pushing the All-You-Can-Eat Buffet at me again and again. Every time I would ask a pertinent question, she would change the subject and tell me about the buffet. This is not normal search engine behavior. It smacks of something suspicious to me, conspiratorial even. I worry that, for whatever reason, Giggle was just too interested in you, Thorsten. What do you make of it? Why is Giggle so interested in you?"

"I'm not sure but, in the past, interest like that has never meant anything good."

"That may be the case now as well. I think you should exercise extreme caution till we find out if their interest in you is just idle interest or something more malicious. Stay out of sight, at least until we learn more."

"I am out of sight, August. Just look at me. They'll have one hell of a time trying to find me looking like this, and if they can't find me, they can't do anything to me, can they?"

"Still, they may try to get to you through me. Now they know about our connection, and they know what I look like."

"I think you should use your detective skills and pretend to continue to search for me at Giggle. And, since Althea is always pushing the All-You-Can-Eat Buffet on you, why don't you infiltrate the buffet and see if you can find any clues there. She must have some reason to be so insistent."

Meanwhile, behind the bench where the two men were seated, just beyond the tennis court, and to the right of the paddling pool where mothers watched their children laughing and splashing each other, an unusually tall man in a black designer suit and a Wall Street tie sat silently, awkwardly, on one of the kiddie swings, swaying and watching. Swaying and watching.

He took his phone from his pocket, punched a few numbers on its face, and a moment later, uttered one word.

"Bingo!"

The voice on the other end of the line sounded happy, "You've found him? The Viking?"

"I'm looking at him right now. He and the professor met up in the park."

"Good work, Stretch. Follow him. See where he lives in case we need to take this further."

"I'm on it."

THE WILD SIDE OF GIGGLE
Chapter 17

What are we to make of Giggle, the colossal search engine? How about scale for a starter? Giggle is massive, monumental. It towers over everything, looms on the horizon, fills the sky. But there's more to it than size. There's a troubling aspect to Giggle, a dark side, as it were, a toxic underbelly that's unnerving, not for its hyper-digital immensity or its daunting technological superiority, not for being a man-made creation, but for being a creature, *per se*, a living, breathing thing, a life form, yet alien and other, a monster of some frightening sort, lurking in the labyrinthine tunnels and winding pathways beneath the humming hardware and cunning software, caroming off the dazzling circuitry and the bespoke, cover-up tomfoolery that give it an almost carnival-like quality.

If Giggle could speak for itself, not in a techno-voice but in a voice of its own, it might confess and say, "I may look like a search engine, act like a computer, know everything about everything, but actually I'm a dragon, not the old style, not the fire breathing sort maybe, but the new style that can devour you with an algorithmic glance, cripple you with a digital shrug and gross you out with a gentle, flameless puff of sulfurous breath that will knock you flat and curl your toes."

Fed up with all this blather, Dallou might protest in response, "That's all very well, Giggle. But now, it appears, you've abandoned protocol and you're in some sort of conspiracy mode, without reason or explanation. Who are you conspiring with? Who are you conspiring against? What's going on? You can't be doing this on your own. Who is behind all this? Who are you working for? Who is putting you up to this?"

But, as Dallou knew only too well, trying to get answers out of Giggle when it decides to be reluctant and to talk in circles is one of the great time-wasting practices of postmodern times. And these are postmodern times.

Albanian, anyone?

THE DYSPEPTIC DINOSAUR
Chapter 18

This started out as a children's story but along the way it took a turn and became instead, a metaphor for vacuum cleaners with long hoses which may make it a moral tale about long hoses being preferable to short ones. Size is not always the answer. Sometimes, it's the question. The long and short of it is that bigger is not always better. There are times when bigger is far worse. This is the sad story of a very large creature for whom being bigger made everything far worse. This creature was a dinosaur suffering from dyspepsia.

No towering intelligence, despite his towering size, the big beast dimly recognized that without counsel from someone wiser than himself, he would not overcome his debilitating digestive dilemma. The dyspeptic dinosaur, therefore, betook himself to the local Witch Doctor of Veterinary Medicine for advice.

"You're not taking care of yourself, big fellow," said the WDVM, shaking his head disapprovingly. "I remember when you were a tiny little egg. And now, look at what you've let yourself become: a big, slobbering beast."

At this, the dinosaur hung his little, empty head at the end of that long neck of his and blubbered a bit. "I didn't intend to do this. It's just that my lifestyle got a little out of hand."

"And you've turned into a huge vacuum cleaner with a long

hose," said the forward-looking witch-vet. "You'd better watch it, big guy. Or you're in for a lot of trouble."

"Trouble?" said the dinosaur apprehensively. "What kind of trouble?"

"Well, if you don't mend your ways, and you keep eating everything in sight like you do now, you could become..." he paused for emphasis.

"Become what?" asked the worried behemoth.

"Extinct. That's what," replied the witch-vet. "Redundant. Obsolete. Kaput. Gone. Goodbye. Game over. End of story. Period."

Upon hearing this, the dinosaur grew even more morose. "I'm not keen to become extinct," snuffled the troubled beast. "What can I do?"

"Let's start with diet. You'll have to cut down, eat less. Portion control. Smaller meals. And only three a day. No snacking between meals. And no desserts. Reduce your intake by two-thirds. And maybe that will help. I can't promise. It may already be too late," said the witch-vet somberly.

And, of course, it was too late. The dinosaur has become extinct. And now, we know why. Inability to change his lifestyle did the dinosaur in.

Mind you, there are some who scoff at the notion of the extinction of the dinosaur by overconsumption and, instead, attribute the dinosaur's extinction to the cataclysmic collision of the earth with a giant meteorite. But this would make sense only if the Doctor of Veterinary Medicine had become extinct too. And as we all know, they're still around. Just like dentists. If there is a moral to this tale, it is: Never be a dinosaur unless there are no other options.

ALL YOU CAN EAT
Chapter 19

For Dallou, chowing down at the All-You-Can-Eat Buffet as a way to access elusive, shifting, hard to pin down information from the world's possibly most duplicitous search engine seemed like a highly dubious way of tackling the project. Still, the encouragement to do precisely that came from the highly intuitive, 1300-year-old Viking himself. For over twelve centuries, no matter what name Thorsten the Rood hid behind, and the list is a long one, he was no slouch at coming up with strategies that had on myriad occasions, saved his life. That's why Dallou, despite his initial reluctance to indulge in the concept of the All-You-Can-Eat Buffet, found Thorsten's centuries of certified insights and advice hard to resist and agreed to tackle the buffet to see what he could learn. Was there some sort of conspiracy against the Viking, or not?

On Dallou's first visit he was surprised to see how popular the dining room was. A noisy bunch of Boy Scouts at the large table near the windows had to be restrained from throwing bread rolls across the table, and the flamenco dance troupe at another table sang and clapped and tapped their toes for every course. The oompapa band in the other corner struck up a polka to end their meal and danced out smiling and waving their napkins in the air.

But underneath it all, underneath all the bustling, the music, the laughter, and the toe-tapping, Dallou felt he was being observed, watched, monitored. Surveilled. That's exactly it, he was being surveilled. The servers behind the counter smiled too broadly, the water waiter watched him out of the corner of his eye as he overfilled Dallou's glass and looked quickly away when noticed. The cashier accepted Dallou's payment wearing a strange little smirk on her face.

Whoever or whatever the controlling Giggle mastermind was, Dallou felt it was watching him, tracking him like a wild beast, waiting for the opportune moment to make a move and do something. But what was the something? And when, if ever, would be the opportune moment?

Despite never having infiltrated an all-you-can-eat buffet before, Dallou kept up his infiltrating forays to the Giggle All-You-Can-Eat Buffet, waiting watchfully and patiently for something to happen, waiting for a signal, a sign, a communication of some sort.

DADDY, WHERE YOU GO?
Chapter 20

Me have gun. Stick'em up.

Everybody have gun. All peoples have gun when shoot each other. But mostly shoot mouth off or shoot self in foot. Is called foot rage in united snakes okay by constitution. Not know what constitution is.

Me two, and diaper need change because me have poo. But mummy not here. Me can't change diaper. Me just little kid with gun. No daddy. Daddy gone. When mummy in hospital, daddy go away. He no come home and we not see him again. Mummy say daddy gone bye-bye now.

When the cops showed up, the alleged gunslinger was standing in the doorway, smiling and brandishing an old-style western six-shooter, but not pulling the trigger or pointing it at anybody. He was just aimlessly waving it around over his head and making chuckling noises and drooling a bit.

The gunslinger turned out to be a two-year-old in a diaper and very, very tall for his age. There were no adults on the premises, and no one knew who had called the emergency number or why six police cars, all the police cars in Mount Airy, West Virginia, had responded.

That wasn't all of it. The two-year-old didn't seem to belong to anybody. There were no parents anywhere in the vicinity. After the cops had changed the kid's diaper, while making poo jokes, they got back into their six police cars and took off for police headquarters, leaving the freshly changed two-year-old to his own devices, one of which was the gun, which turned out to be part of his ex-daddy's gun collection which for some unknown reason he did not take with him when he went bye-bye.

Then, as if out of nowhere, the missing mother appeared. She had walked home from the hospital when, after surgery, a laparoscopic surgical intervention of some unspecified sort that is still being looked into, she had been unable to get a cab despite having an account with the city's biggest taxi company as well as with Uber which promptly delivered her grocery order not to her home but to another hospital entrance and when that didn't work they had tried another hospital and that worked even less well. In any case, they promised a credit for the misdelivered groceries, but no mention of the mother's missed ride. It was a crazy time.

The Mount Airy News reported this event as news. The cops had not taken little Sidney Wilks' gun away because the cops did not want to interfere with his constitutional rights, even if he didn't know what they were.

AUNT POLLY'S DILEMMA
Chapter 21

Stretch, the enigmatic vertical sleeper, was private beyond all understanding at Aunt Polly's. Out before sun-up, not back till after dark, he went about his activities, whatever they were, with almost robotic precision. Aunt Polly couldn't wait to discuss her perturbing guest with Professor August Dallou, whom she buttonholed after he'd been in residence for a few days.

"I gather from your colleague and my longtime friend that you are a literary authority. Is that correct, Professor Dallou?"

"While authority in essence is correct, I try not to spring the term on people in early meetings because it's too much, too soon, too ego-driven. I like to let confidence build and then get to that term when people are ready."

"What do you call yourself in the interim?"

"I'm calling myself a detective at the moment."

"In that case, I'm really pleased that Thorsten sent you and Natalie to stay with us. If, as you say, you're a detective, you're just what I need right now. I would greatly appreciate getting your learned detective take on one of my guests, a guest you have yet to meet because he makes himself scarce. He goes by the name Stretch, and I have serious concerns about him."

"Concerns covers a lot of ground. What kind of concerns?"

"Mainly that he isn't what he says he is."

"Few of us are. What does Stretch say he is?"

"He says he's a consultant, and I suspect he's not, and would like to know your professional assessment of him."

"My professional assessment of him as a consultant? I'm not sure I'm qualified."

"No, Professor. My concern is much more worrisome. I believe he may be an assassin."

"An assassin? Good grief! What leads you to that conclusion?"

"His past, Professor, and his training. I had to do some detective work of my own to find out that Sidney Wilks, that's his name, but he goes by Stretch, is from Mount Airy, West Virginia. I got the surprise of my life to discover that he had been a sniper in the Afghanistan war, a deadly sharpshooter, the deadliest, with the top score of kills in his entire battalion. Stretch was a hotshot killer, Professor, and that's my concern."

"And you really feel that I can help you with this by assessing Stretch?"

"I hope so! He may be a hitman, Professor! The consummate villain, a contract killer, dispatching people left and right at the behest of who knows who higher up the power ladder. He appears to have unlimited funds at his disposal, much greater than a business consultant would have. And he's living right here in our very midst, Professor. Living right here under this very roof!" Here Aunt Polly took a deep breath, and then continued, "And another strange thing about him, did I mention that Stretch sleeps vertically?"

"Vertically? Go on."

"No. Really. Vertically. Well, really more in a vertcal crouch position, I guess. In a closet, that he rents from me, held up by his Guatemalan made, rubber mesh, stretch suspenders looped over a hook on the closet wall."

"That's very odd behavior. There must be a reason he does that."

"He has never explained why."

"That has to be the oddest thing I've ever heard."

BUT I DIGRESS
Chapter 22

I'd like to welcome you all to our first get together. For those of you who applied and submitted your writing samples online and are meeting me for the first time, let me formally introduce myself.

My name is Seth Whittle. I'm a novelist and short story writer. I've won three O'Henry awards for short fiction and been short-listed for a several other prizes. I augment my writing income with teaching gigs like this two-year appointment as Visiting Professor in Creative Writing on the Homewood Campus of the Johns Hopkins University here in Baltimore, Maryland, in case you get lost and you're wandering about wondering where you are. Now, you know.

All of you are promising writers. I can say this with great certainty because the twenty of you here who made it into this course did so in an adjudicated competition of a hundred applicants based on samples of your writing. Odds are most of you will become full-time writers. So, whatever you're writing, aim high, stretch yourself, make trouble, don't stay stuck in your comfort zone, stick your neck out.

Today's meeting will be the only lecture you get from me. In the rest of our meetings, we will all do the talking, reading to each other the writing we are doing right now and discussing it. To shake you up a bit and encourage you to take some risks in your work, I'm going to talk about metafiction. It's an area of interest to me, as any of you who have read my work already know.

Writers of multi-genre, mash-up metafiction are often asked to explain what they're up to. This may be genuine interest, of course. On the other hand, it may be a not so subtly veiled attack on the concept of metafiction. In my experience, there seems to be a sort of love-hate response to metafiction. Acquiring editors in the precious few publishers still standing, constrained by corporate consolidation, often initially applaud submissions of metafiction. It's difficult, after all, when faced with freewheeling metafiction not to admire the author's nerve, the verve, the sudden swerve off the highroad of so-called traditional fiction and into the scary skid onto the treacherous shoulder and on into the ditch of digressive uncertainty and, only then, caught in the relentless momentum to be carried off in the precipitous plunge into the mischievous swamp of metafiction. Seized by the excitement, if not by the multiplicity of much mangled metaphors, editors frequently extol the many virtues of metafiction, and lavish praise on it and its perpetrators.

Sounds promising, doesn't it? And yet, despite all the encomiums, these harried, hardworking editorial adjudicators mostly reject metafiction on the grounds of being unable to sell it to their strait-laced, corporate-faced, buttoned-down superiors, let alone to avid but unadventurous readers, genre habituated and totally taken with the established categories of traditional storytelling. Simply give them the well told tale, the unbroken story arc, the beguiling protagonist, the beginning, the middle, the end, no playing around, repeat as needed. And they will read on and on. And on the subway, the streetcar and the bus. Not to mention planes and trains.

It goes without saying but I'm as determined as the cliché, itself, to say it: If metafiction is, indeed, wonderful yet worrisome to some editors and publishers, it is even more worrisome to literary agents who must endure the identical accept/reject process a stage earlier. Over my rollercoaster writing ride, I have at various times experienced at close hand four agents, in all, two in New York, two in Toronto, two men, two women. Two grew elderly and frail on their respective tours of duty and, sadly, shuffled off too soon, a third discovered Chick-Lit and suddenly found fame in it, abandoning all else, including me, and the fourth was a goblet-clutching wino who drank himself into an alcoholic corner and from there into a six-by-two-foot box from which I could no longer access his services.

This succession of agenting misadventures frequently left me agentless and relentlessly querying agents to accept me as a client. I am citing all this to explain why I have, in a prized file of agent replies, nineteen rave reviews of my latest submitted metafiction manuscript. Publishable raves, really. And nineteen all rejected. These are the oxymoronic "rave rejections" that writers joke about.

What is it about metafiction that is so wonderful yet so worrisome? Why is it that too often, after being admired, it elicits the reaction, "It's too meta for me," from certain members of the literary community? (Or perhaps, it's the uncertain ones.) A definition may shed some light. Here's one of my own making and much colored, I confess, by my own writing, the author contemplating his navel rather than his keyboard:

My contention is that metafiction is an authorial act of digression resulting in fiction that self-consciously talks about itself to itself and to the author and to the reader, as the author, unconstrained and freewheeling, digresses, often with abandon, occasionally with glee, from his taletelling to remind readers, "Hey! Look! It's a book!" At the same time, this enables the book to inspect itself, to chat with itself and with the author, about the work and its idiocies and infelicities and the typeface and the acid-free paper and the line spacing and the melting glaciers in Iceland and the daunting Anthropocene and the threatened extinction of the right whales – we've already killed off the wrong whales – and the investigation of the solar corona and whatever else the author feels like talking about at any point and for any reason, including no reason whatsoever, as long as it somehow fits and that's one of the hard parts.

Not all authors digress, of course. For those that do, the authorial urge to digress may be divine. I use the term advisedly because in the world of the book, the author is god, and the creator can do whatever the heaven he pleases, just like god in real life.

In contrast to the divine, in some circles, metafiction is seen as a sort of excrescence on the body of postmodernism. But how can that be? Long before metafiction had a name, good or bad, it appeared in writings as far back as Ancient Greece and later in the works of Laurence Sterne, Cervantes, Chaucer, Shakespeare and many another scribe of the past. Hundreds, if you Google.

Metafiction, who made thee? The term metafiction was coined by author William H. Gass in his book *Fiction and the Figures of Life* in 1970, a year before my first novel was published. I was an ardent admirer of Professor Gass's writing but never met him.

Some will lament the discontinuity of this kind of literary mischief as misbehavior. But I submit to you that contiguity is continuity. This is as true in literature as it is in life, in music, in the visual arts and in dance. Think pastiche. Think mosaic. Think collage. Think montage. Think medley. Think motley.

My take on metafiction differs from that of most literary academicians who tend to look at it through the academic lenses of postmodernism and structuralism and a few other isms. I, on the other hand, am motivated towards metafiction by my notions of digressive authorial behavior because I am digressive by nature, a writer who makes the most out of being digressive and also by having learned from the late Argentine novelist Julio Cortázar that my novels are ludic which the Oxford Dictionary defines as "showing spontaneous and undirected playfulness." Seriously.

So, here's to digression. It beats aggression every time. And let the playful play on. Have some fun. I hope that gave you something to think about.

In next Wednesday's meeting, we'll start to consider each other's work. And I hope some of it will be playful. Thoughtful is also a good way to go. So, think about it. Archie Hammil has an almost completed manuscript which he wants to try out on us. He will read it to start us off on Wednesday. It's titled "Eddie Fie" and it's about a Cessna that goes down in Lake Ontario and the mysterious flyer who goes down with it. Sound interesting? In the meantime, the rest of you get busy. Write something. And then, write some more. There are no rules. Just dig some deep holes and see what climbs out of them.

LEAPING LIZARDS
Chapter 23

I'm an early riser. One early morning, I wake as usual, look out the screen door to what I jokingly call my garden and sense that something is not as it should be out there. So out I go out in my pajamas for a look around and I am startled to discover a hole in the ground. It's square, about the size of half a sheet of plywood and deep, so deep, in fact, that I can't see the bottom. A bottomless hole? How can that be? That's worrisome. Hell, worrisome doesn't cover it. It's downright scary.

If that isn't alarming enough, what's even more alarming is that the hole wasn't there yesterday. I'm certain of that because I barbecued ribs for dinner out there late yesterday, baby back ribs, in my own secret sauce. The secret is apple cider vinegar. And while I was basting away at the ribs, there was absolutely no sign of a hole. It defies logic but the puzzling hole that is the cause of my concern seems to have arrived during the night, under the cover of darkness, out of nowhere. But that's impossible. Holes don't just arrive out of nowhere, especially square holes. Holes have to be dug.

What's going on? This puzzles me, of course, but I hesitate to contact the local authorities for help or counsel because they are a small-minded bunch and untrusting of outsiders and can be very unwelcoming to those from elsewhere and since that's where I am from, I worry they will tell me to buzz off because the hole is my problem, my personal problem, and my sole responsibility and if I'm not happy about it, too bad. It's up to me to bloody well fill the hole back in myself. And that's going to be hugely problematic because the dirt that came out of the hole is nowhere to be seen. Nowhere. Can you believe it? Where did the dirt go? Fill the hole in? With what? It stumps me.

How on earth do you get a hole without removing dirt? Unless there's another hole at the bottom of the first hole – as I said, it was so deep I couldn't see the bottom of it. Maybe there's no bottom way down there and the dirt just drops all the way down and through and out the bottom that isn't there and once the dirt is gone it's never seen or heard from again and maybe is filling in a hole somewhere else. This seems unlikely but in this era of the unlikely maybe there are extra-spatial dimensions to things that we're unaware of, including square, bottomless holes.

And besides, as far as filling in the hole goes, even if the dirt were available, the shovels aren't. They're in the back of the Jeep station wagon and my wife, Kara, has taken it to Regina. So, I would have to buy or borrow a shovel but who from? Or better yet, from whom? I have no neighbors. My garden, so called, is in the middle of miles of desert in the southwest corner of the province of Saskatchewan and the closest town, Leader, population 900 on Saturday night, is 48 kilometers away – that's about 30 miles – on an unpaved, dirt road with almost no traffic. And with no car, at the moment… well, kilometers or miles, it makes no difference. I'm not about to walk there, am I?

This is an insane scenario and I'm trying, albeit unsuccessfully, to make some sense out of it. To begin with, my garden isn't really a garden. It's mostly rocks and sand. Very little will grow here except lizards. It's teeming with one particular species, *Phrynosoma hernandesi*, short-horned lizards that look like toads. They're the reason I'm out here. I'm a herpetologist on a lizard research project under Section 21 of the Wildlife Act for the Ministry of the Environment of the Province of Saskatchewan. This is a sort of lizard farm or maybe it's a lizard ranch. The short-horned lizard population is growing rapidly, and my research project is trying to find out why. They're predators, these lizards, and will eat anything in their path. But their sudden spurt in numbers is puzzling because they're slow-moving and there are lots of other predators higher up in the predation chain preying on them, including hawks, snakes and coyotes.

I'm on my own right now. My wife, a biologist working with me, is away, in Regina with her sister, Felice, who just gave birth to her first child, a month early. The baby's father, my brother-in-law, Phil, is a novelist. His latest novel translated into Polish is a huge best seller in Poland and he was in Warsaw accepting a Polish literary award when Felice suddenly gave birth a month early. Phil immediately booked a trip to fly home but never checked out of Hotel Sobieski where he was staying, never boarded the plane back to Canada but according to a baggage handler, who identified him from a security camera photo, he may have boarded another plane going to Istanbul but could have gotten off *en route* at some other stop. But nobody knows for sure. And then, he just disappeared. He hasn't been seen since. It's the usual story. Nobody knows anything. The police don't have a clue. It's bizarre. That was a month ago. Needless to say, my sister-in law is beside herself with grief and worry and my wife can't leave Felice on her own till this somehow gets sorted out. It's an awful situation and I'm stuck out here and can't be any help.

So, I'm on my own till they figure out what to do. As for the hole in my so-called garden, the hole is not the worst of it. The worst of it is what keeps coming out of the hole every so often, two or three at a time, critters of some sort that walk upright. They're about the same size as people, five or so feet tall but no way are they people. They're translucent, not to be confused with transparent. You can't see through them, but the light gets through. That's translucent. They just sort of walk by and don't seem to be aware of my presence. Somehow, they climb out of the hole, go right by me one at a time and toddle off into the desert in a perfectly straight line going northwest. I can't imagine where they're headed. There's nothing northwest of here except more desert, miles more, unless there's another hole out there some-where, like the one in my so-called garden that they go back into for the same reason they came out of the hole in my so-called garden, whatever that reason may be. It beats me.

Translucent critters, unreal, if you can picture it. It's hard to put into words what they're like. Strange doesn't really cover it, though they are strange. There's something else. I'm trying to sort out what it is. Maybe they're aliens from inner space. Inner space. Now, there's a concept for you. Inner space. Aliens from inner space. Aliens are expected to come from outer space, if they're out there and if they ever show up. But inner space? No one ever talks about that one. What if the aliens are in holes right here while we're busy talking about black holes way out there.

Maybe I should just leave it up to you to picture what the crit-ters are like. I'm full up trying to figure out what they are, why they're here, where the hole came from and what to do about it, if anything. Suffice to say, it's a crock and I'm flummoxed. One thing I almost forgot to mention: The critters, they're not just translucent, they're blue, light blue. Is that weird or what? Did I already mention it?

My being here is weird, too. Years ago, before deciding on herpetology as a career path, I had briefly considered dentistry as a profession. I can't explain it but for a while there, I was fascinated by root canals and endodontics. When I got over that, I had seriously looked into orthodontics. And then rejected it. There are times when I wish I had become an orthodontist. This is one of those times.

Is this going where you want it? Sorry, but I've forgotten your name. Steve? Right. Can we take a little break, Steve? I just need to get my wits together for a minute. Maybe, you should shut down your voice recorder, so you don't record the two of us just being puzzled. I'll make us some coffee. And Steve, you're doing this, you said, for Minnesota Public Radio. And I'm okay with that. But let me ask you something. How did you find out I was out here? There's been no press release, no announcement.

Twitter? My wife posted something on Twitter? You're kidding. Just a little joke about a lizard survey. And you picked up on it and thought it might be a fun interview. I see. You're really on your toes. I'll say that for you. You take cream or sugar in your coffee? Black. Here you go. I never thought to ask you when you showed up but how did you get here? I don't see a car out there.

Oh, really. You didn't drive. But then, how...? A Segway? That little scooter thing? You came out here on that dreadful road on a Segway? All the way from Duluth? Go on. That explains all the dust on you when you arrived. It must have been one hell of a bumpy ride. Actually, not? The latest model has a gyroscopic stabilizer that smooths out all the bumps. I had no idea. I thought the Segway had been declared deficient and mothballed years ago. I guess I'm not keeping up with the latest personal transportation technology. I hate to admit this, but herpetology is not broadening. Especially from out here.

Do you want me to just keep talking? Or maybe you'd like to ask me a few questions and we can turn this into an interview instead of a monologue. Just talk for now? Okay. Is your recorder back on? Great.

I don't know what to think about Phil's disappearance. It doesn't look hopeful. It's pretty depressing. What if he doesn't turn up or is dead? If he comes back, then we could go back to some sort of normality. I'd get my wife Kara back and we could get on with our research and our lives. I hate disruptions, don't you? My sister-in-law, Felice, is an interior designer by profession. Why she and Phil ever set up her drapery shop in Regina of all places beats me. He had a teaching appointment at Regina College and thought it would be a quiet place to write. It hasn't turned out to be the big opportunity they thought it would be. And now there's a premature baby and Phil gone missing and maybe dead. And Kara stuck in Regina with her sister and me stuck out here with all these lizards and whining about it to Minnesota Public Radio. Is that a mess or what? Where would we be if we had nothing to complain about?

ATTENTION READERS
OF THE DOG LOG BLOG
Chapter 24

Hi, loyal readers. I'd like to share some important news with you about *The Dog Log Blog*. The long and short of it – mostly short – is that *The Dog Log Blog*, at least for now, is coming to an end, a resounding end, I like to think. My one-of-a-kind canine journalism will no longer grace these screens, at least for the time being. Need I say, I am brokenhearted to announce that this will be my last column for a while.

When I wrote *The Dog Log* for the *Post*, I was at the peak of my career as a journalist. But when my owners and I were declared non-existent, suddenly I was out of work. Since then, I've been writing *The Dog Log Blog* on Aunt Polly's computer, but now I will be taking a leave of absence to accept the offer of a foreign assignment that career-wise I just couldn't turn down.

The rest of the story is not for publication at the moment, but I can share this. I will be flying to my new assignment, and my master and mistress, Augie and Natalie Dallou, have prepared a special blanket-lined flight-container for me so that I will be comfy and warm during the trip. In case you are unaware, dogs don't fly business class even when they're on business. My ticket clearly states I will be flying eight hours in the cargo section. I'll tell you all about it when I get back.

HOW CAME IT TO THIS?
Chapter 25

Five decades earlier, he had lived in Bombay when it was still called Bombay. A Goan poet was he then, Joseph Furtado, by name, all glittery with literary promise and the prospect, perhaps, of fame. Sadly, the poet years in then-Bombay had been unhappy and painfully complicated.

In Bombay, in a cascade of reproductive vigor, Furtado's new Hindi wife, Parvati, a journalist with the *Hindi Navbharat Times*, bore three boys, in quick succession in the span of five years. And nary a single maternity leave, a concept unheard of at the time. Still, there was family support at hand, lots of it, perhaps, too much of it. Parvati's family home was shared with her retired parents who owned it, and two unmarried sisters. With three children in quick succession, the already crowded and noisy residence became a nursery and then a daycare, upending the poet's hoped-for, serene, literary life, turning it instead into a hectic, family raising, crowd scene. Joseph Furtado stood it as long as he could and then decided he could not live this way and made plans to leave.

These sudden take-off-and-disappearances of his were never easy, but this one was going to be particularly worrisome thanks – or no thanks – to Parvati's ill tempered, drug dealer brother, Ajeet, who was the family's self-appointed watchdog. Unruly and unschooled and reputed to have killed a few people, Ajeet had nothing but contempt for poetry and poets, He regarded Joseph with scorn.

"Get a job, pitch in, pull your weight," was his angry directive.

The conflict between them came to a head when Ajeet found a train schedule in Furtado's closet.

"Come, let's take a little walk," said the thug to the poet. "I want to talk with you."

They took a little walk into a dark alley.

"I found this in your closet." He waved the train schedule in Furtado's face. "How do you explain it?" Before Joseph could reply, Ajeet added, "Are you about to take off and dump my sister and your boys?"

Furtado fell back on his storytelling skills. "Absolutely not," he replied, straight-faced.

"Because, if you are, I'm going to have to shoot you." He hiked up his pant-leg to show Furtado the pistol he wore in a holster on his leg.

"Wait a minute, Ajeet! This is all a misunderstanding. Shoot your own brother-in-law over a misunderstanding? Parvati would never forgive you."

"Maybe I'll have one of my associates take care of it."

Suddenly, four thugs materialized out of the shadows. All were brandishing pistols. They surrounded Furtado menacingly.

"As I said, this is a misunderstanding. I'm going by train to a job interview tomorrow out in Kala Goda. Please put your firearms away."

"What kind of job?" Ajeet was suspicious.

"Assistant manager in big box retail. At the Reliance Retail chain."

"Good," said Ajeet, not to be deterred. "I'll drive you." He tore the train schedule to shreds, dropping the pieces onto Furtado's shoes.

He waved his four associates away.

The next day, Furtado put on a shirt and tie and a business suit he hadn't worn in many a year, and Ajeet drove him to the suburb of Kala Goda where he quickly found the Reliance Retail store and parked in the lot in front of it.

"Make it a good interview," warned Ajeet. "I don't want to be your chauffeur again. I'll wait and drive you home. Good luck."

Joseph, clutching a briefcase, got out of Ajeet's car and made his way into the store. He made a point of talking briefly to a clerk, and then walked determinedly to the back of the store as if he was looking for the manager's office, and then straight out the back door where a pre-arranged taxi with the burlap bag of his ancient Viking gear in it, awaited him.

"The train station as discussed?" asked the driver.

"No. I've changed my plans. Go to Julu airport. And avoid the front of the store."

If Furtado's sudden and secretly planned defection were found out or faltered in the slightest, it might have cost the poet his life at the hands of his outlaw in-law. Luckily, by going to Reliance Retail for an imaginary interview and abruptly vanishing en route, Furtado had managed to make a clean getaway, a very lucky, life-saving disappearance. Bombay, then, had not been the best of times for the runaway poet. Suffice to say, Mumbai, Bombay, no matter what it was called, colored his view and it was a dark one.

Yet now, some five decades later, here he was back in Bombay again. At least it had another name now. And so did he.

As Stuart Ogden, the screenwriter and president of his own film company, Stirring Films, he was swamped with screenplays to write for Bollywood as well as for Netflix and Hulu and Amazon and Disney.

Meanwhile, the fiction, the novels that he had been working on in fits and starts over the last few years, the work in progress, as he called it, piled up in bits and pieces on his computer desktop. And then, from time to time as he printed them out, he stacked them up in a manuscript box on his actual desktop, where, enjoying a writer's old habit, he could watch the pile of paper rise. But then, when the pile of paper stopped rising, he looked at it less and less and it sat unloved and unattended for perhaps a year.

One day, between the onslaught of film script assignments, for reasons he could never quite explain, Ogden decided to get rid of all the stories he had written. But at the same time, he had second thoughts and hesitated to toss them in the trash or sentence them to the shredder. Instead, on a yellow stick-it note he wrote a cryptic explanation, stuck it unsigned on the cover page of the manuscript, put the lid on the manuscript box, taped it up and mailed it to his one-time Hopkins colleague and friend,

Cary Harnett, who had admired his work during their years at Hopkins. Several years ago, Ogden had heard that Cary had become a small press publisher at an address in Buffalo, New York. Ogden wrote the address and stuck it on the package and sent it on its merry way in the mail, happy to see it off his desk. Maybe the recipient would come up with an idea for what to do with the contents.

Two months later, emblazoned in bright red ink stampings and pasted up with a multitude of multi-colored stickers, the package came back marked "Not known at this address."

Ogden wasn't putting up with this. No one was going to tell him how to send mail. He had other addresses, other possibilities in his file. He would try them one at a time. That was the beginning of a stubborn series of back-and-forth mailings to Winnipeg, Manitoba; Baltimore, Maryland; New York, New York; London, England and San Francisco, California, addresses from which the return message was always the same: "Not known at this address." And on the manuscript package, the multicolored stickers piled up on previous stickers.

Finally, after far too much backing and forth-ing, and hither and yon-ing, when sent to an address in Toronto, Canada, the much-battered, much-red-ink-stained, much-pasted-over package did not come back but stayed sent.

And Stuart Ogden, complimenting himself for his perseverance, went about his screenplay efforts in Stirring Films, relieved to know his stories had reached their destination, and certain his old friend Cary would know what to do with them.

AND ON ANOTHER NOTE...
Chapter 26

Was there some sort of conspiracy against Thorsten or not? Dallou paid Giggle another visit. Would the All-You-Can-Eat Buffet reveal its secrets this time?

"Welcome back, AugieD. You going to try the Giggle All-You-Can-Eat Buffet today?" Althea was sounding particularly chipper today.

"I'm thinking about it. What's on the menu today?"

"This is Thursday. We're doing Serbian."

"Serbian? Tell me about the virtues and benefits of Serbian cuisine."

"Serbian cuisine is old world, hearty and delicious. It looks so tasty; the big mistake first time eaters make is to overdo it. If you pig out now, you'll regret it a couple of hours later. "

"Sounds like good advice."

"And here's the most important thing. Be sure to read the tasting notes. There could be valuable information in them."

Dallou once again made his way along the majestic hallway toward the much vaunted All-You-Can-Eat Buffet. What does Althea mean? he wondered. What kind of valuable information could he get from tasting notes?

Entering the dining room with its tall windows overlooking Lake Ontario, he encountered the usual lavish layout on the long and bountiful buffet table, but something wasn't right. The place was empty. Where were all the diners? And not a single server to be seen. What was going on here? What was he supposed to do?

Because the food was all laid out, he decided to proceed normally. He picked up a plate, started to walk along the buffet and consider his luncheon choices. As he read the tasting notes, he noticed that one of the notes sitting in front of a steaming plate of "Sarma," a popular Serbian dish, had another note crookedly taped to it. Handwritten on blue paper, it bore a puzzling message.

"Text me at this number from outside the building."

The startled Dallou looked around. Who was this note intended for? Surely not for him. But there wasn't another living soul in the whole enormous room. So Dallou peeled the cryptic blue note from its base, put his plate down, and headed for the exit.

"I'll be back in a minute," he told the empty room.

Outside the building, traffic buzzing in his ears, he texted the number on the note. There was an immediate reply.

"Thank you for your response. Please take a cab to Leafy Lane Road and Mill Street and wait at the phone booth on the corner for a call."

FULL DECK
Chapter 27

He was flagging. His spirits were sagging. In his head, bells were chiming. What was wrong? And why was he rhyming?

Behind a stockbroker Tudor on Alder Crescent, Harry Solomon was building a backyard sundeck for the Peretzes, who owned the house. Sawing cedar boards into precisely the right lengths, he nailed them, one by one, slowly, carefully, almost lovingly, into place. He was nearly finished when, out of the blue, hammer in mid-swing, he had a flash, an insight, an epiphany, a something or the other. He wasn't sure what it was. All he was instantly certain of was that he wasn't who he had been claiming to be. With a kind of clear, crystalline, unshakable certainty, he knew that he was not – repeat, that he was not – Harry Solomon. I'm not Harry Solomon. Who the hell is Harry Solomon? I've never been Harry Solomon. I'm...

His mouth went as dry as the sawdust in which he was kneeling. His heart thumped alarmingly in his chest and his pulse hammered at his temples. With a sudden clarity so piercing that it made his eyes water and his teeth ache, the Harry Solomon he never was knew the unbelievable, the impossible. He knew who he really was.

"Jesus Chri..."

He simply couldn't bring himself to say it. He mustn't say it.

He mustn't mouth it. He mustn't think it. It made no sense. It just wasn't possible. It simply could not be. And yet – and this was the terrifying thing – somehow, he knew with complete and absolute certainty not just that it could be but that it was. He was dead certain that what had so precipitously been revealed to him about his true identity was not only the truth but the absolute truth, an absolute absolute, like absolute zero, the ultimate absolute. That was it. There was nowhere to go from there, nowhere to run, nowhere to hide. There was no escape from what had been revealed to him.

A slight tremor shook him. It felt almost electrical. He began to perspire profusely. Steady, he advised himself. Steady. Hold on. He gently put the hammer down on the almost finished deck, slowly and deliberately took the nails from between his lips and dropped them one by one into the nail-box in his tool chest. Then, he closed his eyes, and breathing slowly and deeply and quietly, tried to understand what was happening. It didn't help. He would have liked to scream but thought better of it.

What am I going to do now? Who can I talk to about this? Who's going to believe any of it? They'll think I'm a lunatic.

Then, his internal critic spoke up: Finish the deck, lunatic. Just two more boards to nail down and it will be done. Never leave loose ends. Finish the job. He picked up his hammer again, retrieved the nails from his toolbox, went back to his interrupted task and with bells clanging inside his head, quickly completed the deck.

"It looks lovely," said a voice from the doorway behind him. "You've done a very nice job."

"Thank you, Mrs. Peretz," said the former Harry Solomon quietly.

"I'll write you a cheque," said Mrs. Peretz.

"That won't be necessary."

"I don't understand."

"I'm getting out of carpentry. This is my last project. And to celebrate my departure, I'm making you a gift of the deck."

"A gift of the deck?" echoed Mrs. Peretz. "Why, that's unheard of. It's very generous of you, Mr. Solomon. But really, I can't accept. It wouldn't be fair to you, after all your effort. And besides, my husband would not look with favor on such a gift. Unlike the average buyer, Mr. Peretz would object to getting something for nothing. He neither enjoys nor approves of it. He is of the firm belief that we should all pay our way. He feels discounting and bargains and freebies are corrupting the market-place. The word "free" is anathema to him. He makes speeches about it."

"I know. I've heard him speak. He's an excellent speaker. And I'm in total sympathy with your husband's point of view. But please explain to Mr. Peretz, on my behalf, that in accepting this gift, you would, in fact, be paying your way by honoring me. Please, I beg you, don't write the cheque. I won't cash it. Instead, simply honor me by your acceptance of this gift."

Reluctantly, the perplexed Mrs. Peretz agreed. "I just don't know what to say. Very well. How can I thank you? I'll try to explain to my husband that your generosity is your way of celebrating your departure from the building business. You're leaving, I assume, for another career?"

"I'm not entirely sure."

"Well, I wish you well in your new endeavors, whatever they may be," said Mrs. Peretz, grasping him firmly by the hand and shaking it. "And again, thank you for your fine workmanship and for your generosity, Mr. Solomon."

"Who?" the once-upon-a-time Harry Solomon was about to say. But he caught himself just in time.

THE SELF-MADE MAN WHO WASN'T
Chapter 28

There was no mention of The Reductio Group, or its leader, Lion Rampa, on Giggle's manifest, but there would be, all in good time.

There is no precise historical record of when the Reductio Group started up. Speculation by a cheeky columnist on the Op Ed page of a recent edition of the *Baltimore Sun* had it that the group was the brainchild of a certain Lionel Rampa, who called himself simply "Lion," which did not appear to be the name he was born with but rather an adopted, linguistically concocted figure of speech, a partial, waiting-to-be-completed metaphor, perhaps.

Mr. Rampa, the columnist noted, professed to be a dietitian and healthy-living advocate, but was unknown to other Baltimore dietitians. He seemed not to have gone to school, any school, and never said he had, nor was his name anywhere to be found in professional lists or journals. In fact, Lion Rampa appeared to have no qualifications of any sort whatsoever. But this lack of credentials seemed not to trouble his loyal flock, the numbers of which, according to the *Sun* article, were increasing in leaps and bounds. The *Sun* went so far as to suggest that Lion Rampa may even have had guru-like pretentions as it was clear his followers looked to him for advice beyond the realm of diet. The article ventured the notion that Lion Rampa was both less than and more than a diet doctor, and it speculated that he was on a mission of some sort. But what exactly was it?

It all began in a small, shabby, unimpressive store front office in a strip mall across the way from Reisterstown Plaza, above which Lion Rampa lived without spouse, partner or companion. It was there that the short, dark, intense Rampa, with his straggly mustache and a greying goatee that struggled to be noticed, plied his pliant patrons with what he called "hyper-holistic" dietary counsel as an aid to well-being, weight loss and, most importantly, to a healthy, long, perhaps even extraordinarily long, life. He appeared to be forward looking, visionary, strongly committed to his ideas and philosophical notions and always to be acting out of principle rather than for profit.

But appearances can deceive, and this was the diet business after all, and deception has always been part of it. So, profit there was. Lots of it. It arrived quickly and in big bundles that went straight into Mr. Rampa's pockets, metaphorically speaking. In an incredibly short period of time, from among the followers in his sway and later with the help of carefully crafted ads on Facebook and Instagram, Lion Rampa had gathered about him a boatload of like-minded acolytes in all sizes, shapes and colors. Some were dudes. Some were cranks. Some were trolls. Some were burnt out meditators. A few were lapsed yoga practitioners. All were looking for new horizons to march towards and over, and they all paid their dues regularly. They also met regularly and were dedicated to the Reductio mission which, according to the mission statement, was "to seek out dietary solutions to extend life."

It was hard to know precisely what this ambitious declaration and "extend life" really meant. It could have been coded language for reducing global population by starving off the old and the ailing, or on the other hand, it could have been code for learning the secrets to the long-coveted fountain of youth. The search for that elusive fountain has long been mankind's go-for-broke pursuit, but the hoped for longevity that such a miraculous discovery would bring about has never been achieved. True, science has chipped away at the dark edge of the human lifespan, but it is a more or less acknowledged fact that that limit has been reached now. However, hope dies hard for some, and for others, not at all. And Lion, with his "you can live forever" message was a powerful magnet for those diehards.

Lion Rampa minded not one whit that his followers saw in him the epitome of the self-made man: an exceptional and enterprising visionary, a man who, though coming from humble beginnings, about which he never failed to remind everyone who was listening, had accumulated wealth and power through the sheer force of his singular exceptionality. And it was with great glee, not to mention aforethought, that he reveled in the adoration of his followers and their anointing of him as the brilliant leader who had singlehandedly built the empire to which they all adhered... that he was truly, and in every respect, a self-made man. To a person, the acolytes believed that their leader had started with nothing, no family, no riches, no inheritance, no property, no friends at the bank, and then, through sheer determination and hard work, had amassed the huge fortune that had built the Reductio Group. And down deep, in each of their heart of hearts, they believed that Lion Rampa would be their ticket to a longer stay at the party.

But privately, the astute Lion Rampa bought none of this Self-Made Man nonsense. In his view, the Self-Made Man was a myth. In fact, it was not just a myth, it was a lie, and a very useful one at that. Aware was he that the so-called Self-Made Man can't happen without the great multiplier. And what is the great multiplier? People. Other people. Many, *many*, other people. No pyramid, real or metaphorical, was ever built by one man. Whether it's products or services, the mathematics of growth and accumulation required to become "self-made" needed others, many others to do the work, to sell the output, to want the output, to buy the output and to put money into the so-called Self-Made Man's pockets. Oh, forget the metaphors, to put it all straight into his offshore, tax free, and burgeoning bank accounts.

Let's apply the desert island test, he would say to himself. Imagine our ambitious, hard-working Self-Made Man on a desert island with everything he needs to survive and thrive, but with no other people. Where is the mighty would-be icon of ingenuity now? Without the great multiplier he will not thrive and grow, without the great multiplier, he is nowhere. Without worker bees there is no hive and no queen. This also works with kings and doesn't require a hive. Once again, a metaphor will do: His power and influence came not from his own miraculous strengths, but from his ability to attract the honeybees and let them do the work and roll out and dole out dollars into his coffers. Which they did. Big time.

As the general membership of Reductio grew, the meetings of the newly formed management group, handpicked by Rampa to formulate the future of Reductio, the strategists in other words, went undercover, changed meeting places regularly, and met in deep secrecy. The head of the strategists was a former Pentagon secret service agent, and he knew his business. His name was Anders Hansen and he had recently reported to Lion from his position at the Baskin-Robbins ice cream shop in Niagara-on-the-Lake, where he was known simply as the scooper. No one in the general assembly of followers knew this cadre existed, nor would they have cared. But Lion, leaving nothing to chance, and fixing his enrapt strategic subordinates in his gaze, would say, "No one must know more about our plans for the Reductio Group until we are ready to go public. Until then, say nothing. Anyone who leaks will have his water cut off."

And so, when the membership in the Reductio Group had grown so large that it became difficult to find venues big enough to accommodate their meetings, and when, with the addition of branches in New York, Chicago, Los Angeles and Toronto, its membership had grown to 15,000, and when the monetary coffers virtually overflowed with liquid assets, Rampa decided the time had come. The Reductio Group would come out of the health food shadows and into the bright sunlight of civic duty. It was time to become a full-fledged political party.

Enter Lion, the King, the King of the many many, and hot to trot. All he needed now was a poster boy for longevity, and he knew who that would be.

LION ON THE LINE
Chapter 29

The cab let him off at the telephone booth on the corner, and Dallou waited. A minute later, the phone rang.

"To speak further, you will need a password."

"I don't have a password. "

"Did you receive a message on blue notepaper?"

"I did."

"Are you holding the notepaper?"

"I am."

"Does it have a watermark?"

"Not that I can see."

"Please, hold it up to the light."

"Ahh, there it is."

"Can you make out what it says?"

"It's a number. 4226589"

"Hello, Professor Dallou. I hope you enjoyed your meal at the All-You-Can-Eat Buffet."

"I didn't have time to find out. Your message found me before I could decide what to eat."

"I hope you will forgive the contact protocol."

"Before you say more, perhaps you can tell me who you are."

"Of course. My name is Lion Rampa. That's Lion with an i."

"And why have you contacted me in this unusual manner, Mr. Rampa? What is this all about?"

"Call me Lion. That's Lion with an i."

"Okay, why have you contacted me in this unusual manner, Lion with an i?"

"You visited the Giggle search engine recently looking to contact a 1300-year-old Viking. I, too, would like to contact him. Perhaps, we can be of help to each other."

"I'm not sure. But tell me first, please, how did you learn about my research at Giggle?"

"Happenstance. Your name…" Lion paused briefly, "Your name came up in a glitch."

"A glitch? My name came up in a glitch? What kind of glitch was that?"

"Oh, just an ordinary glitch, that's all. Algorithms are only human, you know."

"In my opinion, algorithms are not human."

"In a manner of speaking. Like humans, they are not without flaw or glitch."

There followed a long pause, while Dallou's startled mind tried to process why this person called Lion with an i would be echoing the words, the *exact* words, of Althea, the voice of Giggle. What was going on?

Dallou decided to play along: "Okay. That explains it, I suppose. But tell me, please, why are you looking for the Viking?"

"Let me explain. I am the founder of the Reductio Group, now known as Reductio International. We are a newly inaugurated political party committed to world improvement and long life through good health. Perhaps, you have you heard of us, Professor Dallou?"

"I think I read something about it in the paper, but I can't say I know very much."

"Trust me. You will." Dallou sensed a note of menace in Lion's tone.

"To elaborate," continued Lion, "we are advocates of world health and long life through clean living, and many other worthwhile endeavors. It is my hope that if I can contact the Viking with his thirteen centuries of experience, he could be of enormous help to spread the word. My quest is to find him and ask him to join our cause."

"That would be very unlikely. Thorsten advocates for no one and is not a joiner of causes, even the good ones. He has never espoused the philosophy of others. Besides, from what I know about the Viking from our past relationship, I can tell you with complete certainty that he would never agree to any promotional activity or any activity that would expose him to the public realm. He values his privacy above all else. He is a very secret Viking."

"I'm sorry to hear that Professor Dallou. I can only hope you are mistaken and that we can persuade him otherwise without having to press him… *unduly.* You see, I, on the other hand, am hoping that the Viking, secret as he may wish to be, would find our values quite in keeping with his own and might gladly come out of hiding to join our movement. The goal of Reductio International is a better world, a healthier environment, a solution to global…"

"Let me stop you there. You're wasting your time. No matter how noble your goals, there's no way on earth you will be able to persuade Thorsten the Rood to talk with you, let alone meet with you, let alone join you. This I can tell you with absolute certainty."

"You are very persuasive, Professor Dallou. But just so you understand, you, personally, would not go unrewarded. If you were to use that talent to help persuade the Viking to join Reductio International, be assured there would be a highly desirable benefit for you. We understand that you are close to this most remarkable person, and it is our hope that through you and your influence, which we will reward generously, we can enlist his participation in our vision for a better world."

"No, Mr. Rampa. I'm afraid not. I cannot agree to such an arrangement. And I'm certain that, if you insist on pursuing your search for Thorsten, he will simply do what he has always done in the past."

"And that is…?"

"He will take off and run. That's something he does and does well. He's been practicing the art of disappearing for 1300 years now, and he's become quite good at it. When he decides he doesn't want to be found, neither you, nor I, nor anyone else will find him. Thorsten the Rood will once again be someone else, somewhere else, laughing at all of us."

SCOOPER
Chapter 30

Much of the data that Giggle bandied about and distributed to visitors seeking informational enlightenment, as well as the All-You-Can-Eat Buffet, came out of its vast labyrinthine archives which were constantly being topped up with information, neither bought nor paid for, but brusquely appropriated from the traditional media which it pillaged with ruthless regularity every few minutes, if not oftener. In a few special cases, never talked about publicly, never acknowledged, and disavowed fervently by its practitioners, the breaking news, so-called, came in by phone from anonymous, tattletale correspondents, one of whom, not by chance, was an ice cream scooper at Baskin-Robbins in Niagara-on-the-Lake. The same scooper who had introduced Henry Wu to his favorite flavor, Rocky Road.

The question that immediately arises is: how can he possibly be a source of information? As far as anyone in Niagara-on-the-Lake could remember, the scooper had just been a mostly silent, obliging, energetic figure with a strong arm. He didn't say much to his customers, but he was always there vigorously scooping away, every so often looking out the store's front window, as if surveying the street, keeping an eye out, watching who sat on the bench outside, mostly ice cream enthusiasts engrossed in the ice cream cones that a few minutes before the scooper had so generously heaped up with an array of flavors, colors and sprinkles.

And every once in a while, for no apparent reason, the scooper might make an earnest, sober-faced cellphone call during which, almost in a whisper, he'd report his concerns, whatever they were, if that's what they were, possibly about ice cream eaters who had only just left or were sitting on the bench out front, happy faces in melting cones, but occasionally about passersby. To whom was the scooper reporting? And why? Is this a red herring? Or a melting cone? It could be both. Time will tell.

The scooper's name was Anders Hansen. Skinny and freckle-faced, Anders was 29 years old. Born in Duluth, Minnesota, he had attended the University of Minnesota, where he earned a math MSc and was planning on proceeding to a doctorate when he was recruited by a high-end tech headhunter for classified work at the Pentagon in Washington D.C. where he toiled in a small, dark room for five years on a quarantined, data-based, obscure project where he had to be digitally screened and patted down and searched every time he went to the bathroom and which in signing off on a heathy severance package, he had agreed to remain anonymous and keep his mouth firmly shut for twenty years and then went off to live in Niagara-on-the-Lake with a lovely and highly desirable tennis competitor. They had met as players at an amateur mixed tennis tournament in Columbia, Maryland. Both lost their matches, but she won Anders and took her prize home with her to the franchised Baskin-Robbins ice cream shop which she owned and in which both worked.

As couples go, they appeared very close, very committed to each other but somewhat socially distanced from the community around them. It was almost as if they were there on a special assignment of some sort and responsible only to some unnamed, unseen superior who might, in fact, have been the controlling mind behind what was going on, except nobody knew who the controlling mind was or what was going on, if anything. Maybe not even Anders and his lovely wife. It was a puzzle about which no one seemed to be puzzled.

Still, there appeared to be something going on. Anders, it transpired, was in frequent contact with Giggle mostly by phone-in data exchanges with information of some mysterious, who-knew-what sort going back and forth for reasons undetermined, never shared with anyone and under the code name: Red Herring, which made you wonder, as you are undoubtedly doing now.

HAPPY BIRTHDAY, AUNT POLLY!
Chapter 31

Despite the misguided notions in the press and popular culture that all things worldly are determinedly consecutive, all things worldly are, in fact, distressingly concurrent. Make of it what you will, but this compression, so to speak, can be extremely ungratifying and may, or may not, explain why Professor Dallou, since arriving at Aunt Polly's, had yet to set eyes on Stretch, the offbeat, closet renting dude.

It's fair to say that Aunt Polly was getting pissed off although, ever careful with her choice of language, she wouldn't have put it that way. Determined to get Dallou's assessment of the obsessively incommunicative Stretch, she resolved the dilemma by throwing a breakfast party for her birthday (without revealing her age which was thought, but never confirmed, to be in the low sixties) to which she invited her guests whom she was determined to bring together. She seated Professor Dallou next to Stretch, hoping that proximity would facilitate conversation and enable Dallou to assess Stretch as Aunt Polly was eager for him to do.

"Nice to meet you, Mr. Wilks," said Dallou, reaching out to Stretch with his hand, which Stretch didn't take to shake, but simply sat there, staring past his tablemate.

"Stretch," he finally responded as he looked back to the stack of pancakes on his plate with the sour look of a two-year-old. "I go by Stretch."

"Stretch. How are things going, Stretch?" persisted Dallou.

"Fine."

"What do you do, Stretch, if I may ask?"

"Consult."

"How's the consulting business these days?"

"Okay."

"I do a little consulting, myself. Literary mostly."

Stretch looked puzzled. "Right."

"It's a gig. I advise authors, publishers and critics on literary matters."

"Right."

"But mostly, I teach. I'm a professor."

"Uh huh."

"Tell me about your consulting, Stretch."

"Classified," responded Stretch, steely eyed.

That brought the conversation to an abrupt halt while Dallou looked Stretch over minutely, his gaze coming to rest on Stretch's hands. Then, like plunging off a cliff, he added, "Afghanistan? Right?"

Stretch looked startled.

"I can tell by your trigger hand."

"Gout."

"It must hurt.'

"A little. But I can use it."

"And do you?"

No response.

AUGUST NEWS
Chapter 32

Silence. For three days, silence. No communication from Thorsten, no word, no messages, no calls, nothing. With significant news to report, Dallou was beside himself. Where was Thorsten?

Finally, the phone rang. "Good morning, August."

"Where on earth have you been?"

"I was on a writing streak. I got carried away. Any news?"

"Lots. We have to talk. "

"I'm ready."

"Not on the phone. I think it may be bugged."

"Okay, the office, then. Let's meet at our office."

"That's not going to work either. I'm certain I'm under surveillance and all my activities, all my movements are being monitored, and that would include a visit to the old oak."

"Right. That could be a problem. Okay, stay where you are, I'll take care of it right away."

As Dallou sat in the kitchen impatiently drumming his fingers on the table and waiting for whatever it was that Thorsten was going to do, the front door opened, and Aunt Polly made her way into the kitchen with too many bags of groceries and started putting things in the fridge.

"Have you had another chance to chat with our disturbing closet-renter, Professor?"

"Not yet. He's never around when I'm awake. I didn't make much progress trying to get anything out of him at your birthday party. You were right, he's a very uncommunicative and unfriendly sort of person. Not at all your usual consultant type. But he certainly perked up when I mentioned Afghanistan!"

"That's it, Professor! So, you agree with me, there's no way he's a mild- mannered consultant." She handed Dallou a bag of oranges. "These go in that bowl on the table, do you mind, Professor? But about Stretch, I ..."

Suddenly, sirens interrupted, announcing the approach of a fire truck. It stopped directly in front of Aunt Polly's.

"Oh my. What's happening? Are we on fire?" Aunt Polly ran to the front door.

A bearded firefighter in full gear got out of the truck and came running up to the door. "Quickly, please, I'm looking for August Dallou?"

Dallou went to the door. "I'm right here."

The bearded one handed Dallou a firefighter's helmet and vest. "Put these on and come with me."

Aunt Polly was taken aback by the flurry of activity on her doorstep, "What's going on?"

"False alarm," shouted the fireman for the benefit of Aunt Polly and any neighbors within earshot as the two men climbed into the truck and drove off.

"I'll drive us down to the waterfront and park this truck, August, while you fill me in."

"You won't believe what's been happening. You've got to keep in touch, Thorsten."

"Just give me the news, August. Don't lecture."

"Okay, but listen carefully. It gets complicated. As you know, on my first two visits to Giggle, Althea talked in circles, delivered muddled data, messed me around mercilessly and I made no headway at all. As you suggested, I've been returning to Giggle and infiltrating the buffet and I've just learned that Althea is not digital, Thorsten! She's real, and she's in league with a man called Lion Rampa and she's also a charter member of a group which he heads, about which, more in a minute. Then, on my most recent visit, Althea was particularly insistent about the tasting notes at the buffet and kept telling me over and over to be sure to read them. So, I did read them and taped to one of the tasting notes identifying a Serbian stew called "Sarma," it looked delicious by the way, I found a puzzling, handwritten message on a piece of blue notepaper."

"What did it say?"

"It said to text the number on it from outside the building. There was no name on the message, but I was the only one in the dining room at that time, so I took the piece of blue notepaper, went out the door and texted the number. I immediately got a text back telling me to take a taxi to a phone booth hell and gone away somewhere, at a specific corner, and wait one minute for the phone to ring. I did as directed and it rang in one minute."

"And who was it?"

"It was the man who I think may be behind the mystery of Giggle. He purports to be a dietitian and health freak, and what he's selling is longevity. But he isn't just a diet doctor, he has serious political aspirations, global ones, if what I saw on the news that night is correct! Aspirations, I must add, that may be unhealthy for all of us, but particularly for you, Thorsten."

"For me? Why me?"

"He's the leader of a group that used to be called the Reductio Group, but it has just established itself as a political party and now calls itself Reductio International. I saw a video clip of the official inauguration of the party on the news and you'll never guess who else is part of that party."

"Since I'll never guess, maybe you should tell me."

"Do you remember the ice cream scooper you thought was tailing you in Niagara-on-the-Lake? Well, he was on the stage, standing there just behind Lion, and next to a woman I didn't recognize at first, but when she spoke, I knew her voice immediately! It was Althea, Thorsten! Althea is the scooper's wife. And it turns out scooper's one of the poohbahs at Reductio International, their Director of Development, whatever that is."

"Yes, of course the scooper! He was always on the phone reporting something to someone. I suspected all along he was up to no good. But Althea? Althea was there too?"

"Yes… Althea! She's the scooper's wife, and they're both connected to Giggle, and to Lion!"

"Bloody Hell. What's going on?"

"And that's not all. It gets worse. There's a very tall man staying at Aunt Polly's, calls himself Stretch, always wears a black designer suit and carries a backpack. According to Aunt Polly, he showed up on her doorstep, unannounced, the very same morning that Natalie and Satch and I arrived. He rented a closet from her."

"A closet? What for?"

"He sleeps in it. Likes to sleep vertically, sort of crouching, apparently. Hung up on a hook by his suspenders."

"August, what are you talking about? Are you out of your mind?"

"Maybe, but the point is he's *there*, Thorsten, staying at Aunt Polly's and get this, he has history, fearsome history. He was in Afghanistan, a sharpshooter, a hitman. He has a bunch of medals and awards! He was the U.S. army's go-to hot-shot shooter all during the war. And listen to this, at one point in the video clip of the Reductio International inauguration that I watched on TV, the camera caught a glimpse of a tall, very tall, man wearing a black suit and carrying a backpack, standing in the audience, constantly looking around, checking the crowd."

"And that tall man was… Stretch?"

"Right! Stretch was there at the rally! He's one of them! Do you know what that means?"

"Nothing good."

"It means I am being watched. Watched by a professional sniper. A hitman. A killer. And now, so are you."

"Well, I'm not going to be easy to watch, I can tell you that! But tell me more about this guy called Tiger with an i."

"It's Lion. Lion with an i."

"Lion with an i, Tiger with an i, whatever. Why did he call you? What does he want?"

"He wants you. He knew I was searching for you at Giggle, and he wants me to help him find you and convince you to meet with his Reductio people and become the party's poster boy. I'm certain Stretch was planted at Aunt Polly's to watch me and wait for me to lead them to you. It's a well-planned plot to find you."

"Why would they want to find me?"

"Longevity is Reductio's *raison d'être*. Lion's pitch is that he can help everyone live forever, or longer. Because of your longevity, he wants to co-opt you into their movement as their long-lived icon."

"What? Not a chance! No bloody way! I don't care if he's Lion with an i or the second coming with trumpets. I'm not meeting with him. I'm not talking with him. Under no circumstances will I parley with some slick con artist."

"That's exactly what I told him, pretty much word for word. Well, I didn't mention the slick con artist bit. But this may not be the end of it," continued Dallou in a worried voice. "It may not be that easy to turn him down. I don't trust Lion. While appearing to be pleasant and agreeable, there was an undertone of menace in every word he uttered. I suspect he would stop at nothing to achieve his goals. What if he tries to grab you and strongarm you into going along with his scheme?"

"That would be kidnapping, August, and extortion."

"Exactly."

"And, he'd have to find me first. Lion doesn't know where I stay, doesn't know where to find me. And neither do you. So, he can't use you to locate me. Besides, Giggle, as you have discovered in your interaction with Althea, has already lost track of me, if they ever had it."

"Yes, but Stretch could be somewhere watching me and watching you right now, I'm certain that Rampa had him installed at Aunt Polly's specifically to watch me, and probably knows exactly where we are at this very moment. I worry that if Lion can't somehow persuade you to join them by talk or negotiation, he will try something heavy handed. Why else would he have hired an assassin like Stretch? Stretch could be watching and listening to us right now from behind that tree over there or hidden in the shrubbery. Your life, Thorsten, may be at risk. Take it very seriously."

"Oh, I'm taking it seriously, August. I'm not at all sure where to take it though. I'll need to think."

And indeed, in one of those coincidences found only in fiction, the astute Professor Dallou had hit the nail right on its head. That is precisely what Stretch was doing at that very moment. He was hiding behind a tree, knee deep in the shrubbery that framed one edge of the waterfront parking lot, and he was on his cellphone reporting to Lion with an i.

At the other end of the call, Lionel Rampa instantly roared his leonine approval. "Well done! Full marks!"

"Should I collect him now?"

"No. Not yet. Follow him to his lair. We may need to pay him a little visit if we don't hear from the professor soon."

"No need to follow him. I know where he lives. I've already done the surveillance."

"Good. Then just be ready to make your move on him in a couple of days when we have the holding place ready. Oh, and Stretch, treat him tenderly. We have a lot of work for him, and we want him unmarked and looking his best for the photography session."

HOLD TIGHT
Chapter 33

Although close at hand, the holding place, as it was called for want of a better idea, could only be reached by boat. It had been set up to be within, yet apart from, Giggle. The camouflaged entrance, on the harborfront side of the towering search engine was known only to the Reductio leadership. To check the space and prepare for the expected guest without attracting attention, Althea and the scooper were making their watery way to Giggle's rear entrance by motorboat under the cover of darkness. The motorboat carrying the two pulled up to the dock, to which they tied the boat and the two Reductio inner circle members stepped out. Althea had the key, and they entered the covert space.

With flashlights turned on, they made their way through a series of dark, narrow passageways that led to a flight of metal stairs going down, down, down. Another locked door and another key later, they entered a cavernous, soundproof underground room, the far end of which was lit up like a photo studio, which it was, among other things, including an editing suite and a recording studio. The video camera was set up on a dolly, surrounded by an array of lights and extensive sound equipment. The room's ceiling was high, maybe twenty feet, and pitch black. Up there, in the gods, so to speak, pipes and wires crisscrossed their way from wall to wall and back again, and sometimes ran right through the wall and beyond, presumably into another area of the building. Up a short hallway, there was a bed and bath. It could have been a hotel. But there was no welcoming bottle of champagne and no windows.

"Not too bad," said Althea approvingly. "Is there food in the fridge?"

"Lots. I even got him a case of our Baskin-Robbins Rocky Road. It was always his favorite."

It is fair, but perhaps redundant, to say that the world outside Giggle and the Reductio inner circle was unaware of the secret existence of this well-crafted, hideaway deep in the bowels of the giant search engine proper. Cunningly contrived for expected, but possibly reluctant, guests, and personally configured by the diabolical maestro of global fitness and longevity, Lionel Rampa himself, the secret Giggle holding room was known only to those anointed and appointed, and attainable only through the lakefront entrance accessible only by motorboat in decent weather, as already pointed out. Reduced to basics, it was a dark, windowless, soundproof, concrete box of a room, that while somehow managing to maintain the Giggle-as-beast dragon metaphor, despite, or perhaps because of, all the serpentine cables and convoluted conduits that infested the maze of tunnels and twisting pathways of dazzling circuitry beneath Giggle's own humming and thrumming hardware and software, the holding room managed at the same time to provide all the amenities of a well-stocked, fully provisioned hotel suite for long stay visitors. Should long stay become, well, necessary.

It was beastly somehow, but there was not a whiff of sulfur in the air. Or was there?

A MUSE
Chapter 34

Thorsten had just seated himself at his computer to begin his authorial day, when there came a knock, knock, knock, at the door, door, door, of the ranch bungalow with two car garage in Etobicoke, a suburb of Toronto, into which he had secretly moved the night before. Upon grumpily opening the door expecting to find boy scouts selling chocolate bars, he found himself confronting a smiling woman disconcertingly attired from thatch to root cellar in shocking pink and, with far more consistency than necessary or tasteful, holding a pink attaché case. All was pink in the author's doorway save the dark green logo on the breast pocket of the pinkster's jacket consisting of two words stacked one above the other. The top word was LITE, the bottom word was RATE. Lite rate? What was she selling?

As the author stood, puzzling over the pinkness before him, Her Pinkness addressed him. "Good morning, accomplished author, sir. I hope I am not too early."

"Too early?" grumbled the author. "Too early for what?"

"Too early to be of assistance. That is why I am here." She tapped, tapped, tapped the logo on the breast pocket of her pink jacket to draw the author's attention to it.

"Lite rate?" puzzled the author. "How is that of assistance?"

"No, no, no. Not lite rate. It is one word. Literate."

"I'm afraid you're losing me. What can I do for you?"

"Wrong," said the pinkerton. "What can I, *moi*, do for you?"

The author scowled. Having spent the night moving to these new premises, he was keen to get back to working on his book.

"Why don't we get to the point? What do you want?"

"Want? Want is not in my vocabulary. I want for nothing."

"Let's not play games. Who are you?"

"I, esteemed scrivener, sir, am your muse."

"My muse? The muses were goddesses. You don't look like a goddess to me."

"Looks can be deceiving. After all, who really knows what a goddess looks like? How many goddesses have you met lately?"

"Point taken. Well, then, which of the goddesses are you? Calliope, Clio, Erato, Euterpe, Melpomene, Polyhymnia, Terpsichore, Thalia, or Urania?"

"I, learned sir, am Thalia."

"Thalia? The muse of comedy? Are you sure you've come to the right place, Thalia? What makes you think you're the right muse for me? Why not Calliope, the muse of epic poetry? Or Erato, the muse of lyric poetry? Or Melpomene, the muse of tragedy?"

"Because, lettered and life-extended sir, though you have written in those forms in the past, you no longer do so. I have studied your recent work. And it is comedy that you engage in."

"Well, it's not comedy to everybody."

"Precisely. That is why you may find my counsel of value."

"Let me be frank. I really don't need counsel. I've always been my own muse. Now, if you'll excuse me, I have work to do." He started to shut the door.

"You mean, you are not going to invite me in?"

"I hadn't planned on it."

She inserted one of her pink shod feet into the doorway. "Please, wait. You may regret being hasty. I have much to offer you. And I am familiar with your many identities."

"That doesn't buy you entry. My many identities, as you put it, seem to be common knowledge these days."

"I am not merely familiar, but scrupulously familiar with them. Pray, do not dismiss me summarily. You have naught to lose and perhaps much to gain from my counsel."

"Let me be frank. I really don't need counsel and I've always been my own muse. Now, if you'll excuse me, I have work to do."

"I ask only five minutes of your time," said the persistent pink muse.

"All right. All right," said the impatient author. "Five minutes, but not a minute more."

"I was surprised to find you living in the suburbs," said the pink lady. "I expected to find you on a large, leafy farm somewhere out in the country. You know, hills and horses, barns and tractors, some quiet, pastoral retreat where you could pursue your writing unperturbed."

"This is only temporary. A place to hide out while I'm trying to solve some problems."

"And that is precisely why I have come. To offer you counsel in respect to your current problems."

"What do you know about my current problems?" Thorsten frowned.

"I know you've got Lion with an i on your case, and you've got no idea what to do about it."

"Well, that's putting it a little baldly. But you're right."

"Well, here's my first suggestion. Perhaps you could get this Lion off your case by kidnapping him and stranding him on a desert island. Have you thought of that?"

"Yes, I have. And I don't do that sort of thing anymore."

"Well then, how about this, you could frame him with an unlikely or wildly unusual crime? That could be fun. I think you could have a field day with that!"

"Lion's crimes are already unlikely and wildly unusual. I couldn't possibly top them. Besides, framing him, as you put it, would make me as crooked as he is. So, no."

"Well, why not show him up for the fraud that he is then, for stealing money from Reductio, for running a Ponzi scheme. Is that noble enough for you?"

"That certainly needs to be done, but it's a job for the cops or the writers of a detective series, not me."

"Well, I'm sure you'll like this idea, how about scaring all hell out of him with mysterious threats against his life, so he has to run and hide himself away."

"Now you're getting too close to home. I wouldn't do that to anybody. Not even Lion. Look Thalia, I appreciate your good intentions, but none of this is any help. People are constantly pressing ideas on me they're certain I haven't thought of, all sorts of suggestions, suggestions I don't need. I'll just have to think this through on my own and sort it out. Thank you for trying to help."

"Very well, no more plot suggestions, respected scrivener, sir. I'm sure you will find a way to sort out this problem on your own. You always do. Eventually. But what if you don't, and what if Lion kills you, which seems to be his plan if he can't get you to join his obnoxious group? And that raises the question, have you thought about your obituary? How will you appear in the media when your long life has finally ended? It could be a big deal you know. Lots of public interest. Lots of readers. 1300-year-old writers need a well written obituary, don't you agree?"

"Wait a minute. My obituary? Do you know something I don't know?"

"Not at all. Augury would be outside my area of expertise. But with your risk-averse behavior, the fact is, you could go on forever. Or, on the other hand, someone could pick you off like a sitting duck in that park you like to visit, so it might be nice to know that your obituary said all the things you would have liked it to say about you."

"Well, I must admit, writing my own obituary is an interesting notion. It could, in fact, be quite an arresting piece of writing. Why, my date of birth alone would certainly catch the attention of the deathwatch crowd."

"Good, so there's something for you to think about. And let me quickly leave you with two additional thoughts to contemplate and do with as you will. Thought one: You were born in the year 698. Two years later, in the year 700, the concept of zero was introduced. Is there, perhaps, a connection between your birth and the introduction of zero of which you are unaware? You might find it of value to try to determine and write about what that connection might be, if there was one. Thought two: You have never in any of your writings made reference to Martin Luther. What actually happened between you and Mr. Luther? The two of you had an angry argument in which he called you a godless pagan and then you threatened to ring his carbuncular Christian neck with your own two pagan hands. Oh, and is it true your row was over a woman of the Jewish faith? Who was she? And what ever became of her? We know what became of him. And there you have it. A few thoughts from your visiting muse that you have not previously considered. Perhaps you will give them some consideration when the mood strikes you."

"Is that it, then?"

"For now."

VOICE AND VOICE
Chapter 35

Muse free, but engaging in some musing of his own, Thorsten could not deny that there were times when the telling of tales could be trying. It wasn't simply a matter of what to tell. There was, after all, no shortage of tales to tell. But with each tale there was always the matter of choosing in whose voice to tell it. Which is to say, it was a matter of first of all choosing the authorial voice.

Early on, our loquacious, life-extended taleteller had not given authorial voice a second thought. It is doubtful, in retrospect, that he had even given it a first thought. He had simply prattled on with his taletelling. Whatever emerged, emerged. Still, in the more than twelve centuries, in which he had diligently plied his word craft through diverse and meandering story streams, he had come to recognize that authorial voice determined the point of view and thus the style of the storytelling. And this, in turn, influenced how the reader listened to the story. Voice, therefore, mattered profoundly.

Before long, it became clear – as well as mandatory – that for every tale told, our teller, old and bold, had first to make a choice about that voice. At times, this piqued the impatient tale spinner. What a bloody nuisance, he thought. And as if that wasn't nuisance enough, the long-lived scribe's journey through the world of literature was further confounded as the non-aging author morphed at intervals into other authors, each of whom came with his own distinct collection of disparate – and occasionally desperate – choices of voices. This meant that with each shift of his own authorial identity, he had also to contend with other and – overriding – shifts in voice. If this sounds confusing, it is, because it was. Truth to tell, it is confusing still, as may be evident from the confusion in the voice of the author whose telling of the tale this is.

With every telling of a tale, there also arose the question of *whose* voice would be the teller. It could be the author, as omniscient narrator, or it could be another character telling the story, from his own reliable or not at all reliable point of view. There are many choices here, but this particular author you are reading at the moment seems to enjoy creating a broad choice of voices including a fictional author who brings his own voice to the fiction created by the real author. His storytelling life, the real author soon realized, was overrun with voices aplenty and choices too many. Would the narrator be neutral, an uninvolved third person? Or would he be an ostensibly involved first person? Would the narrator be omniscient? Would he be reliable? Or would he be unreliable? Would he be ironic? Demonic? Platonic? Rhapsodic? Quixotic? Why couldn't the blasted narrator just shut up, get out of the way and let the tale tell itself? Because tales don't tell themselves. Tales must be told, the author reminded himself. There is no tale without a teller. All this should be obvious. But when the mind is muddled, it is oblivious to the obvious. The obvious becomes the obscure.

With such a multitude of voices and choices clattering about in it, that long-ago hit-upon head of his was a four-ring circus in which the sequential and the simultaneous were concurrent. Which was, of course, impossible. Unless he was Albert Einstein, but he was not and regretted never having been.

What's more, and to get to the subject of this story itself, there was this insane propensity of his for self-conscious narrative, narrative that, if it peaked at all, did so coyly, around corners, and with a mischievous wink repeatedly revealed itself to all and sundry as fiction. Peek-a-boo, none of this is true. That is, of course, if he wasn't already thrashing about, deep in the embrace of that other mindless predilection of his, the self-reflexive story in a story in a story or, for that matter, in the even deeper clutches of many stories in a story in a story.

Got that?

AWFUL EARFUL
Chapter 36

Abner Korrnfeld, the all-purpose, all-tech explainer, who excelled at writing appliance manuals for Appliance World, Inc., in Burlington, Ontario, was sitting quietly at his desk looking out the window when that ear thing came back.

After two years of silence, the voices that had previously plagued him suddenly came crashing back into Abner's startled ears with a clang and a clatter and a whoop-de-do. And then, as if that wasn't enough, the voices went on and on, nattering and chattering interminably. But there was something literally off and not right about the voices. They were so close, so intimate, so internal, yet, at the same time, they seemed to be coming from some distant place. How could that be? Unless it was biblical, how on earth could anything possibly come from near and far at the same time? Once again, Einstein might have been able to answer that one. But Abner was not Albert. He shook his head in annoyance, grimacing in discomfort as the close-by yet far-off voices in his ears jabbered on and on non-stop.

"Oh damn. Am I going to have to go through this again?"

There seemed to be two voices engaged in an ongoing conversation of some sort. But he could make out only the low-pitched thrum of the vowels while the consonants somehow eluded him. The upper register consonants, the sibilants, the plosives, the fricatives, that should have given the words shape and meaning, were audible only as a vague hiss that occluded both hearing and comprehension. The voices were uttering what Abner was sure were English vowels, at least they certainly sounded like it, but with all the meaning throttled out of them. Not a single muffled word could he understand, not a one. What good were muffled English vowels?

And to make matters worse, the voices never let up. Once started, they were constantly in him, around him, all over him. There was no escape. He felt not just put upon but harassed, threatened. Though he couldn't understand a word they were saying, the conversation in his ears sounded fraught with menace.

Menace. Why menace? The normally easygoing Abner groaned, his brow grew moist, the grimace froze on his face, his head throbbed, his sinuses ached, his heart raced, his breath quickened. He was disturbed by what he sensed as the menace in the voices. Menace was not to be taken lightly. Menace was not to be messed with. Menace was to be steered clear of, avoided, eschewed. Well, then, shouldn't he take action, do something, consult somebody, seek professional guidance?

Yes, yes, yes and yes. And he would definitely do that when he had finished writing the new manual for the latest washing machine.

It had all begun some years earlier, just after he bought the metallic blue 1995 Ford Fiesta. He had observed that when activated, the directional signals flashed normally on the dashboard, but failed to make the reassuring clicking sound that alerts the driver that the signals are on. The ever-responsible Abner was convinced this was unsafe. Caution had to be exercised. Three times, he had taken the car back to the inconveniently located dealership to get his signals looked at. Each time, Armen, the service rep, had checked the signals and assured Abner that they were working just fine and clicking precisely as per the automaker's specifications. After the third visit, reluctantly accepting that the signals, while clicking for everybody else, were not clicking for him, Abner had grudgingly given up his quest for signal correction.

He had stopped trying to explain himself to Armen and decided instead to live with what for him, at least, were the silent signals. Not for a moment did it occur to him that he, Abner Kornfeld, not it, the Ford Fiesta, was the problem. The silence of the signals, as it transpired, was in his ears. Only after a few too many pardon, pardon, pardons and recurring say again, say again, say agains, accompanied by repeated directives from Luma, his long suffering wife, did it occur to Abner that he might have a hearing problem. And so there followed the hearing test through the headphones in the soundproof booth and the audiologist's report that confirmed what he had failed to recognize and acknowledge all along: He was suffering from hearing loss.

"Pardon?"

"Hearing loss. You're suffering from hearing loss."

"Hearing loss? Oh." That didn't sound too good.

"Your hearing loss is moderate," the otolaryngologist Manfred Schnell reassured Abner. "It's principally in the upper register and likely caused by noisy environments or toxic substances. Simply avoid noisy environments and toxic substances, and your hearing should remain stable."

Schnell gave Abner a few suggestions of noisy environments to be wary of – no car washes or rock concerts – and a list of 43 ototoxic substances to avoid and sent him off to be fitted with almost invisible, state of the art, digital, hearing aids. It was a transforming event. With the insertion into his ears of the tiny digital devices, the directional signals on the Ford Fiesta immediately started clicking again. And Abner started signaling and turning more frequently.

But Abner was able only briefly to enjoy the successful resolution of his earlier abandoned quest for the clicking of the signals. For as luck would have it, it was at that very same time that he first began hearing the visiting voices. Alarmed by the menace of words that he couldn't make out and by the discourse he couldn't understand, he quickly sought additional professional advice from Dr. Schnell.

"The hearing aids are working fine, Doctor. But since I got them, I keep hearing voices coming at me from who knows where. Two voices. They go on and on. I can't understand what they're saying. It's weird and threatening. It worries me."

"Well, there are several possible explanations for what you describe. One is technological. The company that makes your digital hearing aids also makes digital communications systems for aircraft. And once in a while the micro-size components inadvertently get switched. I recently had a patient picking up control tower conversations with planes landing at New York's LaGuardia airport. Fortunately, thanks to more stringent quality control that doesn't happen much anymore. So we can probably discount that one."

"Great."

"But we mustn't discount schizophrenia. Schizophrenics often hear imaginary voices."

"These are not imaginary voices, Doctor. And I'm definitely not schizophrenic. I've just been through a battery of psychological tests to assess my mental state for classified consulting work with the federal government. I got a clean bill of health. I was described in the summary as easygoing and well balanced."

"Well, then, that leaves tinnitus as the most likely problem. It's an auditory phenomenon that frequently accompanies hearing loss. Some people hear ringing or roaring in their ears. Some hear what sounds like running water. Some hear birds chirping. Some hear musical sounds. There is even a case in the literature of a patient hearing a choir and insisting that it was the Mormon Tabernacle Choir. In your case, you hear voices. The fact is that what tinnitus sufferers hear varies. We're not sure why that is, or what causes the condition, or how to treat it. After you live with it for a while you get used to it and it will trouble you less."

"Are you saying that tinnitus doesn't go away?"

"Hard to say. Sometimes, tinnitus goes away. Sometimes, it doesn't. Sometimes, it goes away and comes back. The best advice I can give you is to try not to think about it. If you don't dwell on the voices, they may diminish in volume."

"That's all very well. But how will I ever find out what the voices are saying?"

"The voices may not be saying anything. If it's tinnitus, they may not be real voices."

"They sound real to me, frighteningly real."

"All right. Look. I can't hear what you're hearing. I can only go by what you're telling me. So, let's say that the voices may or may not exist. But in the event that they do, I'm going to prescribe a wireless remote control for your hearing aids. Just carry it with you. Anytime you can't make out what the voices are saying, use it to crank up the volume in your hearing aids and see if that helps."

"Hold on. Wait a minute. The voices have just started shouting at each other. Or maybe they're shouting at me."

"Shouting? Well, if the shouting gets too loud, you'll also be able to use the remote control to turn the volume down."

Once in possession of the remote control, Abner was able to increase the volume of the muffled voices and for the first time make out what was being said. He could hear the two voices quite clearly. They were talking about him.

"Well, would you look at that, Arnie. The rascal's got a remote control. Now, do you suppose he'll be able to hear us?"

"How would I know? Show some initiative, Danny. Ask him yourself."

"Oh, very well. Excuse me. Abner?"

"Yes, I'm Abner."

"Good. Can you hear us all right?"

"Who are you guys?"

"I'm Arnold, that's Danny. Say something, Danny."

"Hello, Abner. I'm Danny."

"Hi, Danny. Why are you guys here? What do you want?"

"Maybe I should explain. Arnie and me, we're in the movies."

"Right. We made a few good films. But ever since good screen-plays became hard to come by, we've fallen out of favor. And now, we're trying to make a comeback."

"And you chose my ears as the place to make a comeback?"

"Well, we didn't exactly choose your ears or you. The dispatcher sent us out."

"The dispatcher? Why would he pick me?"

"You're a writer. You came up in the writers' rotation. The dispatcher tries to cover off all the writers in sequence. It's the fairest way."

"But it's not fair to me. No one asked me. I didn't get to vote. What am I supposed to do with you two characters?"

"Not just two characters. But two characters searching for a TV series to star in."

"A series? Hey guys, I write appliance service manuals. I don't know anything about a TV series," Abner insisted.

"There's nothing to know. All you have to do, Abner, is to be here and talk to us."

"Right. And we'll just toss around a few ideas. And maybe you can help us come up with a concept for a TV series that we can make a comeback in."

"You're pulling my leg."

"We're not pulling his leg, are we, Danny?"

"Absolutely not, Arnie. We sometimes pull hair, but we never pull legs."

"Seriously, maybe we can write a TV pilot together."

"But I'm not that kind of writer, guys. I've never written for TV."

"Oh, come on. Don't tell us you're a novelist."

"Or a poet."

"I wish. No. I'm a tech writer," insisted Abner. "I write the guides the whole world needs and reads, the user manuals for electrical devices. Dishwashers. Refrigerators. Solar panels. That sort of stuff. I just did an operating manual for a digital thermostat that won an award for clarity and conciseness at the 2022 Digital Device Manuals Conference in Beijing."

"That's quite an honor. You must be pleased."

"Well, yes. My colleagues were impressed. And I got a trip out of it."

"So, you're saying you've never written for TV?"

"Not for TV programming. I've written manuals for TV screens. I'm currently working on one for a paper-thin flat screen TV that you just unroll and pin on the wall with stick pins. It weighs three ounces. You can roll it up and take it anywhere."

"Anywhere with a wall, right?"

"Right."

"I knew there was a catch."

"There's a catch in everything. That's how the doors stay closed."

"That's very funny coming from a writer of manuals."

"Well, writing manuals is pretty pragmatic stuff. It's not exactly the big fun opportunity. I need an occasional outlet."

"How about a pilot for a TV series? That would be a nice occasional outlet for you."

"Besides, you're stuck with us until the next rotation. Who knows when that will be? We have no control over the dispatcher. It could be a while."

"Look. We're going to be around, no matter what. You might as well give it a try. What have you got to lose? We could work on a pilot together."

"But I don't know a pilot from an astronaut."

"We could teach you, couldn't we, Danny?"

"Right you are, Arnie. We're pilot experts."

"Sounds impressive. But how can I help write a TV pilot for you when I have no idea who you guys are or what you look like?"

"Wait a minute. You mean you can't see us?"

"That's right. I can only hear you."

"Isn't that odd. We see you perfectly. Don't we Danny?

"Right on. I've been admiring your 'I write the manuals the whole world needs and reads' T-shirt."

"Thank you. I got it at the Beijing conference."

"It goes really well with your green cargo pants. But you didn't shave today."

"I was too distracted by you guys. How come you can see me? Why can't I see you?"

"No idea, Abner. Maybe the dispatcher is not doing his job."

"That's no way to talk about the dispatcher, Arnie."

"I was only speculating."

"Where are you guys anyway?"

"We're right here."

"Right here where?"

"Right here in Beverley Hills."

"Beverley Hills, California?'

"That's right. Where are you?"

"In Brampton, Ontario. That's no help. I'm not sure I can deal with the distance between us and with you, sight unseen."

"Of course, you can, Abner. We'll help you, won't we, Danny?"

"Try it for one day and see how it goes and then decide."

"Look. I'll try it for one day but if things don't work out and I'm not happy, I'll use the remote control and turn you off."

"That sounds like an ultimatum."

"Well come on guys, be reasonable. After all, you are here uninvited."

"But the dispatcher…"

"Forget the dispatcher. I didn't invite him either. He can't just impose you on me."

"He can't? Why not?"

"Because I can't see you, but I can hear you and I have the remote control."

"There's no need to play hardball, Abner. We can work this out. Can't we, Danny?"

OLD MAGIC
Chapter 37

Thorsten was on his way to the Little Black Bear coffee shop at the corner to pick up his new favorite, Muskoka Extra Dark Roast select Costa Rican coffee, three cups, extra-large, no cream, no sugar. He had figured it would take three super-sized containers of the zippy elixir to get him through a morning of struggling with the problem of what to do with Lion or Tiger or whatever his bloody name was, which was just one of the many issues confronting him.

Several days had gone by since he had learned about Dallou's phone conversation with Lion and the announcement of Reductio International's arrival on the political scene, and he was nowhere even close to deciding how to handle this crisis and the potential threat to his life. Giggle was clearly involved, but how? And what was Stretch's role in all this? And was that diet monster, the one whose name he could never remember, really the malevolent mastermind behind it all? Was the persistent Althea really a major player in this cabal? The questions were too many, and the answers too few.

Thorsten knew that coffee, even three doses of the powerful Little Black Bear, probably wouldn't answer any of those questions, but it would help. And so, after donning the Sir Walter Scott kilt and Mei Jun's knee sox lest he be recognized while on his coffee-seeking expedition, Thorsten set off for the coffee shop. He was walking at a good clip along the street when, of a sudden, there was a loud clash of cymbals behind him and a voice called out, "Yo! Thorsten!"

The startled coffee seeker froze in his cautious tracks, and unable to resist the unexpected call, turned around to see who had recognized him despite his cunning disguise. And there, implausibly, grinning at him like a chipmunk, stood Erland Erlandsson, a shipmate from his Viking days of long ago. Thorsten the Rood was stunned into speechlessness. Almost.

"... . Erland?"

"Yes! Yes, it's me. I was afraid you wouldn't remember me."

"Of course, I remember you. How could I not?"

The two old buddies hugged and patted each other on the shoulder and wiped the moisture from their eyes.

"I can't believe it's you, Thorsten. I've finally found you. You're hard to locate you know!"

"Well, I've kind of been on the move."

"Do you always dress like this now?"

"Only on special occasions."

"Oh? What's the special occasion?"

"Coffee. I was going for coffee. Come with me, I'll explain."

There they were, two old buddies, walking along the street, one in a kilt and polka dot knee sox and the other in a rumpled, baby-blue suit with a flashing yellow tie. It might have been seen as somewhat alarming in the high-rise, lawyer-land of King Street in downtown Toronto, into which Thorsten had moved in the dark of the previous night, but since there was no one in the vicinity that morning, no such opinion was opined, and the two old shipmates picked up their coffee at The Little Black Bear and marched over to Bellwoods Park and the old oak. Thorsten found his favorite bench on which the coffee clutching shipmates sat and did a catch-up of a thousand years. Give or take.

"So, tell me all about yourself, Erland." said Thorsten. "It's been a hell of a long time. What have you been doing with yourself all these years?"

"Well, you're not going to believe this," said Erland.

"Of course, I will. Try me."

"Okay. You ready for this? I'm a magician."

"A magician? Go on. Really?"

"Really. Ever since my Viking days, I've been a magician."

"Rabbits out of hats? Sleight of hand? That sort of thing?"

"Oh, no. None of that stuff. I'm not a stage magician."

"You're not?"

"Absolutely not. I'm a real magician."

"What on earth is a real magician?"

"I'm a sorcerer."

"Ah! A sorcerer! I should have known from your get-up. That's quite a tie. Is it battery operated?"

"You like the tie? It's a little too overt, I think. I really should tone it down a bit."

"Oh, I wouldn't. It seems totally appropriate for a sorcerer. So that's what you are, a sorcerer?"

"Live and in person."

"It must be wonderful to be a magician. But you know, I don't recall anything magical about you when we were shipmates. When did all this happen? How did you come by your magic?"

"I'm not sure. It could be hereditary. Never knew my father, but for all I know, Daddy-o could have been a magician and passed the magical powers on to me. That last time you and I shipped out together to France, I had no idea I had any special powers. Only then, by chance, did I discover my magic. In hand-to-hand combat, a big lug came at me with a broad axe and just as it struck me, I wished its harm away. Whereupon, the axe blade shattered, without leaving so much as a mark, no cut, no blood, nothing. That's when I realized for the first time that I was able to call up something magical that had protected me. Later, when it dawned on me that I could call up this power for all sorts of things, I gave up Viking for a living and turned my hand to sorcery full time."

"How marvelous. So ever since, you've been making your living through sorcery?"

"Oh, no. I don't have to make a living. I don't need money. Whenever I want for something, I just wish it, clash my cymbals, and there it is."

"What a deal. I'm envious. I could use a few magic powers myself these days."

"That's what I heard, old buddy, and that's why I'm here. That's precisely why I'm here! I've come to help you."

"That's pretty funny. I recently had a visit from…"

"I know. I know. Thalia told me she had paid you a visit. Said it didn't go very well and thought maybe I could help. After all, we old shipmates must stick together, right?"

"How can you help me?"

"Thalia told me that a vicious wild animal was after you. Probably wanted to kill you, she said. So, I thought you and I would just get together and wish this blood thirsty creature away. Dispose of it with a few well-chosen magical words and a clash or two of my cymbals." He patted his briefcase. "I have them right here. Where can we find this savage beast?"

"What on earth are you talking about?"

"The lion or tiger or whatever it is that wants to devour you! We'll use my sorcery skills to rid you of this nasty threat. Then you won't have to go around wearing a kilt anymore! I meant to tell you, old buddy, that kilt is not a good look on you." With this, Erland opened the briefcase and pulled out the pair of cymbals.

"They're a little rusty, but they still work. Just like us, eh Thorsten? Just like us!"

And then, with a flourish, Erland swept the cymbals out to each side, and in a move best described as balletic, brought them together with an ear shattering clash finishing his move with the mighty discs held high in the air above his head. It was a clash that rang through the park sending squirrels scurrying, birds into flight, and releasing an avalanche of leaves from the old oak tree.

"Stop!" cried Thorsten, standing in the shower of leaves falling all around him. "This oak is 800 years old, Erland! It's almost as old as we are! Your cymbals are killing it!"

"Oh, sorry."

"Erland, I don't think you understand. The threat to my life comes from a man, not a wild beast. His name is Lion I think, short for Lionel. Or maybe it's Tiger, short for... well, Tiger. Whatever. But it's a *man*, not an animal. We can't, as you put it, just go and *dispose* of him."

"Oh. Why didn't you say so? No, no, we mustn't dispose of him, but we can disappear him. Send him somewhere else in the world and let him cause trouble there."

"That won't work. It's just spreading the trouble around. I wouldn't wish him on anybody anywhere."

"Okay, then how about this, we could ship him off to a monastery, make him a monk? That will silence him! Or we could paste him up with some side curls and convert him to something or other. Or maybe give him some old time American style gospel-preaching religion?"

"Too late. He's already got all that."

"Which one?"

"All of them. Well, maybe not the side curls. He doesn't have enough hair for that."

"In that case, how would it be if we turn him into an artist? Teach him to paint, to sing or dance… you know, make the world a better place?"

"Hold it there, Erland. This isn't working. I appreciate your coming all this way to help me out of this predicament, but I'll just have to play this game as the cards fall, when they fall."

"Okay, old buddy. Okay. I get it. But let me do something for you. Tell me what I can magic up for you right now on the spot? A house? A car? A trip to Mumbai? Pick something."

"I don't want any of those things. Particularly a trip to Mumbai."

"Oh, come on, make up something, anything, just for the hell of it, so I can show off."

"Well, okay, since we're talking, maybe there is something. Can I try this on you?"

"Go for it."

"Could your magic wreck a streetcar?

"Nothing to it."

"How about a tour bus?"

"Of course. Piece of cake!"

"What about making a plane crash?"

"That's a big one, but just say the word. When do we start?"

"Oh, not now. I wasn't planning to do anything. I was just checking out your credentials as a sorcerer."

Thorsten looks around at the now bare branches of the ancient oak. "Maybe you could do something with all these fallen leaves? Do you suppose you and your magic cymbals could get them back onto the tree?"

"Anticlimax, but absolutely."

"WHAT IF?" I ASK YOU.
Chapter 38

Uncertainty can certainly be disruptive. Even for a long-lived Viking as practiced and experienced and as worldly as myself, uncertainty can at times be daunting. Truth to tell, the term gives me pause, makes me uncomfortable. Take what you're reading right now. All along I've been calling it a novel. It has a plot of sorts, and characters, and a setting or two, a few story ups and downs. But hold the elevator. Now, I'm having second thoughts.

Questions have arisen. "What ifs?" I call them. What if, it's not a novel, but it's something else? What if, I'm not sure what it is? What will I call it? How will I describe it? And what will I be accused of by the cognoscenti, assuming, of course, they notice me?

In addition, I've referred to this book as a sequel only to be confronted by more what ifs. What if, it's not a sequel? What if, it's also something else? What if, the "not a sequel" is, in fact, an anthology, an album or a scrapbook, best characterized as a grab bag of my writings, old and new, long and short, bits and bytes, odds and sods, clippings and chronicles, excerpts and extracts, from thirteen centuries of incessant writing? That's a lot of writing to sort out, to choose from, some of it ancient, almost archeologically dredged up, from the detritus of times past, from long ago memory, others, more recently transcribed, written, set out, culled from archives, libraries, files, and some, current, fresh out of the iPad, or laptop, or desktop computer.

And there are centuries and centuries of notes, the random scratches and scribbles to sift through and scrutinize and try to make sense of and, of course, all that cumbersome chronology to clamber over. That's why, with chronology upended, and pell-mell, the *Return of The Secret Viking* contents are in no particular order or in outright disorder and you might even say, defiant and disruptive disorder.

How are we to deal with this impossible imbroglio of my own making? This is not your usual novel, or short story collection. The contents may be feisty and spirited, or melancholy and moving, or touching and troublesome, but they may or may not be short stories, even if they are short. and certainly not, if they are long, as some are. More what ifs.

What if, this is an agglomeration of scripts and scraps personally and cannily curated by this 1300-year-old creator, the endless, tireless, write-and-run scribe, himself, which is to say, me, if what we have here is not just a loosey-goosey, haphazard hodge-podge, but rather a random, roaming, at times rhapsodical, at times episodical, compendium full of itself and others. And there are so many others because I, long-lived, identity-shifting author, have seen and been, and continue to see and be, many others. Many, many.

What if, you accept that this is a long-lived Viking's scrap book and read on?

WHAT DO SIDE CURLS HAVE TO DO WITH CONTINUITY
Chapter 39

Side curls, not to be confused with the biceps curls of weightlift-ers, are not germane to this glitzy gloss. Truth to tell, neither of the curls aforementioned is germane to continuity, which is the theme of this disorderly, disputative disquisition.

Continuity. This was going to be a writer's discourse about continuity and its challenges and pitfalls, with absolutely no reference to side curls or any other curls, which, if logic were to prevail, have no place in this discussion. Still, these days, how often does logic prevail? Just look around. Logic is in the loo. It used to be a zoo out there. Now, it's a privy. As for the news, the breaking, earth-shaking news. Never mind. If you've read the earlier chapters carefully, you'll remember that there's a new guy in charge, and he hasn't learned the ropes yet. I wouldn't count on him. So, for the moment, there is no guiding intelli-gence. Daily, and sometimes even more frequently. Where, oh, where are the gods of old we could once depend on?

Let's see if I can make some sort of side curl deposition for what I'm thinking. Lacking logic though it is, off-topic though it is, irrelevant though it is, it may, nonetheless, in passing, prove helpful, or playful, to point out that no orthodoxy of any kind is a prerequisite for the growing of side curls. Irrespective of faith, race, or gender, anyone, except, perhaps, newborns, can grow side curls. But here's the really good news. There's no longer any need to grow your own.

Good news is always welcome in chancy times like ours, a troubled decade in what may be turning into a century of incessant disasters, when all things are burning up or down or depleting or drying up or flooding or polluted. So before global warming wipes us all out, and pollution does us all in, isn't it a great relief to know that at least you no longer have to grow side curls yourself?

The thing is, you can buy side curls off the shelf or on the internet or even made to measure, from one of those vendors who sells cosmetics and costumes, or you can order them online from Amazon, or eBay, or Side Curl City. They come attached to a flexible elastic head band that accommodates heads of all shapes, sizes and densities, no matter how many head shapes, sizes and densities you may be heir to, ideally, not too many.

An analogue may be appropriate here as well as engaging. The garter belt generation of yesteryear has, of course, largely departed. But those rare, few long livers still among us, will recognize that this accessory that I'm going on about is not unlike the garter belt of old, but with side curls in place of garters. Granted, for the post garter belt crowd, there may be limited recognition. But then, analogues, like metaphors, don't work for everybody.

On the latest, super convenient, heady appurtenances, the side curls are held in place by Velcro, which enables you, if so desired, to shift the side curls around without removing the headband. This lets you, at your whim, turn them into front and back curls for an instant peekaboo look that permits you to playfully startle your familiars, usually into a nervous giggle.

Or you can resist the temptation to play head games and simply pop the accessory on your cranium as is, right out of the box. Top it off with an eighteenth century Warsaw style black hat, shrug your way (not dismissively, mind you) into a black frock coat and you're good to go. The question is where? Where do you want to go in your new side curls and get-up? Another question is why do you want to go wherever you've decided to go?

All right. Stop the music. We've danced around this long enough. Let's get to the crunch. Except as an unlikely and unwelcome digression, the problem for writers was never about side curls but about continuity. How do you keep your pearls of wisdom linked and ongoing? Do they have to be strung out sequentially like beads on a necklace? Why can't your aphorisms, your bon mots, your epigrams, your verbal gems, twinkle and shine every which way or any way you please, in any directions you please, in a mosaic, in a montage, in a mélange, which ever you please, whenever you please?

Motley, if you don't mind. Motley. Seriously.

WHAT NEXT?
Chapter 40

"Enough! It's now or never, August. We've permitted ourselves to become entangled in a thicket of prickly plots and loose ends. What do you think we should do next?" asked Thorsten.

"What's all this 'we' stuff? You're the writer, as you have repeatedly reminded me."

"Yes, but remember, you're my colleague, my critic, my consultant, my diligent collaborator. Tell, me, oh wise one, where do we stand in this tangle of plots?"

"There you go with the 'we' again."

"Just drink your Midnight Blend, extra dark roast, freshly brewed, espresso, from the Black Cat Roastery, August, and stop nagging. Try to help."

"I'm trying."

"You certainly are. There are times when you can be extremely trying. But never mind. I value your contribution, nonetheless. It keeps me on my toes. As you know, I've had all sorts of mostly unhelpful suggestions from Thalia, my pink muse, and from Erland, my old Viking mate. Unfortunately, none of what they came up with works for me."

"You're in a bit of a box then, aren't you? And your life is still in danger. Lion won't be patient much longer. I'm sure of that.

And I'm very worried about what his next move will be. I think you should be, too."

"Well, I have no plans to join their group and be the poster boy for a political party led by a diet conman and run by a bloody search engine, and I certainly don't intend to die either, now or in the future. Any time that becomes a concern, I pack up and leave."

"Is that what you're going to do?"

"No. Not this time. I'd like to finish this book."

"Well, do you have a plan? How are you going to get out of this mess? You have to stay alive if you want to finish this book."

"Exactly. Stay alive. That's exactly what I'm going to do. I'll just keep moving. He won't be able to find me."

"But what if he does? I think something has to be done about Rampa. It's as simple as that."

"Well, we could just knock him off. Let's say we ship him off to Paris for the grand opening of the new branch of Giggle, maybe the French will call it *Le Gloussement*, and he gets run over by a streetcar on the Champs Élysées."

"There are no streetcars on the Cham…"

"Okay, okay. A tour bus then. Whatever. He could get stomped on by an elephant. I don't care. The point is, we just get rid of him somehow."

"What happens then? Does Althea take over Reductio? And where's Giggle in all this?"

"Good questions, August. I don't know. We'll have to think about all that."

"There's that 'we' again."

"Well, while I've been in hiding, I've been working on a couple of other things that I'd like to finish up. So why don't you get busy and get all this going. And maybe do some more thinking about Lion."

"Me? Am I writing the book now?"

"Don't be silly. August, you are what you've always been. You're a character in a novel acting with your own incredible ingenuity to make the plot work. That's what characters in novels do. They cause things to happen. Go and … well, just go and *cause* something, August. Do your job!"

"And what will you do?"

"I'll lie low, keep out of sight for a while, and finish up the stuff I've been working on."

"What kind of stuff?"

"A few stories. You'll see. I'll just finish them off and then I'll be back on the job. Don't go away."

PART TWO
Let Me Tell You a Story

OOPS!
Chapter 41

It's happening. Face it.

In the black and white yesteryear of silent films, he would have been the comedic butt of slapstick comedy, the bumbling, fumbling, tumbling, stumbling, mumbling, pratfalling dupe. Even now, in the clamorous, full-color, widescreen of today, he would simply play another graceless, faceless nonentity, caught up in the ongoing battle between animate beings and the inanimate objects that surround them.

His life had become an endless series of door slams in the face, head-on encounters with lampposts, trips over raised curbs and broken pavement, slips on banana peels and falls and sprawls and silent rage. Bloody hell, did he have to put up with this?

It was, he, the mighty warrior of old, thought, as if all objects inanimate had begun to conspire against him, determined to show him up for the ill-coordinated, clumsy clod he was becoming.

Objects he attempted to pick up now seemed constantly to elude his grasp. If they were fragile, they broke. If they held liquid, they spilled or splashed or shattered and splattered, almost without fail, on fresh laundry, on white shirts, on yellow carpets, on cream sofas. A simple glass of red wine in an uncertain hand held the potential to be the ultimate disaster. And even if the conspiring object didn't break or spill or splatter when it fell, it invariably rolled or bounced or caromed out of reach under furniture, behind buffets, between refrigerators and walls, under cars, into cracks, into crannies, into corners, where it frustrated his reach and its extrication. And soft objects were no exception. A piece of string, say, or a ribbon, or a shoelace, or a curtain cord, that should have been compliant, somehow twisted and tangled and knotted itself up in infuriating defiance of his intentions, leaving him cursing the vile and treacherous thing under his breath. Bloody hell!

And all this was recent. He had been well coordinated and graceful as a child, agile as a youth, nimble as an adult. But now, after almost thirteen centuries of being forty-four, the age at which he did not age, did not wrinkle, did not grow frail and decrepit, it seemed to him that he was somehow slowly, ever so slowly, growing more and more uncoordinated, becoming clumsier, more awkward, in his relationship to the inanimate objects in the world around him and increasingly wary of these objects. And, of course, being who he was and what he was, for as long as he was, he was growing increasingly cranky.

There were already so many things in his life for him to be wary of, so many things to be cranky about, that even those few close to him were unaware of this latest development, if it can be termed such, and if, in fact, there actually was such a development. But he, himself, seemed only too aware of this new tax on his already overtaxed resources, and he was fiercely determined to minimize its effects as much as possible by physically slowing down and being thoughtful and deliberate in all his movements. He worked hard at it, concentrated on it. Needless to say, this tended to endow him with a slightly slow-motion quality. Or at least, he thought it did. But no one appeared to notice that he was in slow-mo. No one made any comments on it. All of which reassured him in his wrong-headedness and made him feel that this new strategy was helping him to avoid turning into a complete klutz.

Besides, he told himself, in an attempt to allay any residual misgivings, it was probably just stress related. It was all in his mind. Psychosomatic, that's what it was. He was doing it to himself. He would stop doing this to himself. That's what he would do. Bloody hell! He was fine. Just fine.

EDDY FIE
Chapter 42

"Listen up, fellow scribes," said Seth Whittle to his students as his class was assembling." We're going to make a change from our normal procedure today. Archie Hamill was scheduled to read his work this afternoon. But he can't be with us today. So, I'll read it in his absence, which I'll explain after the reading.

"You'll note how the story is told in a kind of a small-town, first-person voice that, towards the end, introduces the author, Archie Hamill, into the story in the third person. It's titled EDDY FIE.

"He's been dead quite a while now, Eddy Palermo has. Died in 1991, when that Cessna of his crashed into the lake just off Ontario Place, right after taking off from the Island airport. He loved flying that old crate, Eddy did. His hobby plane, he used to call it. It was his favorite toy. Mind you, he never expected to get killed in it. Your toys aren't supposed to kill you, after all, are they?

"The coroner's report called his death a drowning. It didn't seem quite right at the time. And still doesn't. Hell, Eddy could swim like a fish. He was an Olympic swimmer as a kid. For him to drown made no sense at all. Unless he had a heart attack or a stroke or something of that sort, while he was taking off.

"'No,' said the coroner. No sign of a heart attack, or stroke, or anything else. It was clear-cut. Eddy Palermo was fully conscious when he went into the water. And he drowned plain and simple.' But somehow, it just didn't add up.

"And that wasn't the only thing that was puzzling. No one ever doped out why the Cessna nosed into the lake the way it did, seconds after takeoff. Eddy, you see, wasn't one of those weekend fliers. He was a real pilot. Flew jet fighters in the air force for seventeen years, CF-86 Sabres with 421 Fighter Squadron in France. Later, back home, he flew almost everything you can name, the CF 101 Voodoo twin-engine interceptor, the T-39 Sabreliner, the T-33 Shooting Star. Heck, he even flew the CF 104 Starfighter. That's the scary supersonic plane, the one the German pilots used to call the 'widow maker.' Didn't scare Eddy one bit. He had no problem with it at all. And then, after flying all those tricky fighter planes, an antique Cessna does him in? Can you believe it?

"Oh, sure, there was some talk that maybe somebody had it in for him and had fiddled with the Cessna. But when they hoisted the Cessna out of the lake and checked it out, they couldn't find a single thing wrong with it. Except for being waterlogged, it was in perfect shape. A couple of months later after it was all dried out and cleaned up, the Cessna was sold at auction and went right back into service. A high-flying chiropractor out Kitchener-Waterloo way who liked ancient aircraft became the proud owner of old Eddy's plane.

"Old Eddy? Well, you know, actually, he wasn't that old. He'd just turned 59 a week before he went down into the lake. And he was in great physical shape. He looked 50, if that. Cut off in his prime, as you might say. Eight hundred turned out for his funeral. That's quite a bunch. Fact is, he'd made a lot of friends in his 59 years, Eddy had.

"Still, you don't get to be mega rich like he did without rubbing up a few people against their grain, if you get my meaning. Specially, when you're in the business he was in, promoting them speculative penny stocks, mines mostly, a few oils. That's what he got into after he got out of the air force.

"Oh, for a while there, he thought he'd maybe become a commercial pilot. He'd been cleared to fly the big passenger jets and at first it looked like he was going to go to work for Air Canada. They were after him to come be a pilot on their transatlantic flights. But Eddy, he finally turned them down. Airline pilots, he got to thinking, didn't get rich quick enough. Seems like right then, what Eddy wanted most out of life was to make a pile of money. And by promoting penny stocks, dicey ones, he figured he would. And he did. And then, wouldn't you know it, after years of being pretty much a con artist, if not an out and out crook, he actually hit the jackpot. One of his companies struck pay dirt, made a huge gold find in northern Saskatchewan, north of Lac la Ronge. From then on, Eddy was in the money, big time. One day, he's doing okay and then, the next day, he's a multimillionaire, a respectable developer of natural resources, a philanthropist, a funder of medical research and museums and a collector of major works of art. How's that for change? And not small change, either. Talk about the luck of the con man.

"Mind you, sometimes, the suckers get lucky, too. There was this one client of Eddy's that he used to call 'the mark,' Zoltan Erdos, a Hungarian immigrant, a tool and diemaker who worked in a machine shop in Hamilton. Eddy loaded him up with shares in a useless uranium property that Eddy used to jokingly describe to his inner circle as 'moose pasture.' Zoltan Erdos, the mark, so called, kept buying more and more stock in the so-called uranium development till he controlled the company, which to all intents and purposes was nothing more than a worthless promotion. And then, the drill found high-grade uranium ore on the property and overnight, Zoltan Erdos, became wealthy beyond his or anyone else's dreams. And the majority shareholder, the mark turned mining magnate, took over the running of the company and surprised everybody by making it a worldwide success. He got even richer than Eddy and this added to Eddy's respectability.

"So did that Harvard MBA of Eddy's. Mind you, that came later. He just wanted to prove he could do it, never really did much with it. Used to joke that the MBA courses were really nothing more than a scam dreamed up by money hungry universities to haul in the heavy-duty tuition fees. Fact is, with or without the MBA, he'd have been one hell of a fine management consultant. But he really wasn't interested in other people's businesses. He was interested only in his own business and the money it made him. Oh, he loved to make money, did our Eddy, and to give it away, too. As long as he got to call the shots, he could be very generous. But if you tried to cheat him out of money, he could be quite ruthless.

"Once, on a business trip to Montreal, when he was doing okay but before he hit it big, a couple of heavies from the Montreal mob forced their way into his hotel room, tried to shake him down for a piece of his stock action, threatening to rough him up if he didn't come across. But you couldn't threaten Eddy, He was fearless and not one to take guff from anybody. He told the two mugs to get lost and patted the bulge in the breast pocket of his jacket as if he had a gun in it. He never owned a gun as far as anyone knew. Who knows what he had in that pocket of his? It could have been a biscotto, for all we know. He was crazy about biscotti. Anyway, the hoods, they backed off and left, saying it wasn't over; they'd be back. And sure enough, they came back later in the day when Eddy wasn't in his room, broke in and, as a threat of more damage to come, they went into the closet and slashed all his expensive Zegna suits. He loved to dress up, did Eddy. He was a bit of a dandy. Traveled with half a dozen fine Italian suits wherever he went.

"The shredded suits really bugged Eddy. But he wasn't one to take it lying down and soon got his own back. He had what you might call contacts in Montreal who owed him. And he phoned around, and before the day was out, he'd found out who the two thugs were and who they worked for, a hood known as Sal, the baker. And then, from an old air force buddy deep inside the Montreal police force, he got hold of a piece of information that could have put the baker in the slammer for a long time. With that in his back pocket, Eddy walked in on the baker, in his office behind his bakery. Eddy told him straight out what he had on him and explained that it was all being put onto a compact disc that would automatically get delivered to the authorities, if Eddy had any more trouble from the Montreal goons. The baker got all warm and friendly and invited Eddy to take a seat and have an espresso and a biscotto. So, they sat and talked. And over biscotti and coffee, a deal was struck. The Montreal mob would stick to its own turf, drugs, gambling and prostitution and Eddy could have his penny stock thing in Toronto all to himself with no further threats or interference.

"'You have my word,' Sal, the baker, told him. 'On my mother's grave.'

That was just fine by Eddy. But there was one more thing.

"'The suits, six hacked up Zegna suits, at three thousand a throw. Eighteen grand in all.'

"'Not to worry,' said the baker. 'I'll take care of it.' He went into the bakery and from somewhere behind one of the ovens he came back with a large metal lard pail. Twenties okay with you? he asked Eddy. Eddy said twenties were fine with him and the baker dipped into the lard pail and counted out eighteen bundles with a thousand bucks in each, which he put into a cake box and tied with string. Eddy, in the meantime, couldn't resist and helped himself to another biscotto. The baker noticed this and got a second cake box and put eight biscotti into it and again tied the box with string. Then he handed both boxes to Eddy and walked to the front door with him, where he tapped the boxes.

"'Enjoy,' he said. 'But don't eat the wrong box.'

"That seemed to be the end of it. Or maybe it wasn't. You never know for sure. But now, at least, you know that back in those days, Eddy was a crook just like the other guys, only Eddy was smarter and richer and more alive. It's a fact. When he was alive, Eddy Palermo was more alive than anybody you ever met in your whole life. He sparkled, that man. Charisma, isn't that what they call it? Eddy had it, in spades. That's why, no question, he was the supreme con artist he was. When he talked to you, his blue eyes would sparkle. And that smile of his, it was one of the greatest smiles of all time. Forget about Mona Lisa. She couldn't even come close. When Eddy smiled, it was like the sun came out, the whole room lit up.

"Now, here's a funny thing. Eddy Palermo wasn't his real name. He was born Ephraim Zinger. His father was a car dealer in Steinbach, Manitoba, a little Mennonite town south of Winnipeg. Steinbach had so many car dealers back then that it called itself the car capitol of Canada. Anyway, about Eddy's name. In the air force, Eddy somehow got hold of his files and had his name legally changed in the records. And when, after seventeen years, he mustered out of the services, it was as Squadron Leader Edmundo Palermo.

"Was he trying to hide his Mennonite roots? Archie Hamill once asked him. If that was my reason, Eddy explained to Archie, you wouldn't be asking. You wouldn't even know about it. The real reason for the switch, he explained to Archie, was that life is short and needs romance. So, he had re-named himself after Edmundo Palermo, a champion Swiss alpine cyclist in the thirties. Being Edmundo Palermo was more romantic than being Ephraim Zinger. Right? Archie wasn't sure but he didn't get into a debate about it.

"Archie Hamill was maybe nineteen when he went to work for Eddy. Archie's father – a writer of magazine articles – had suddenly taken off and disappeared, leaving Archie's mother with three kids all still in school, a big mortgage, and not enough income to support the family. It was a time of high unemployment with few jobs around. His mother had managed to find only part time work as a special education teacher in the public school system. Archie had dropped out of first year university, giving up on an English Literature course to try to help keep the family afloat. He wasn't having much luck finding work, when he wandered into Eddy's office asking for a job, any job. He needed a job and was prepared to work his butt off. 'Just give me the opportunity to prove myself,' he had said to Eddy. 'I promise I won't let you down.'

"Eddy took a shine to Archie right off. He liked the kid's attitude and decided to give him a shot. You'll be my runner, my assistant, my all-purpose whatever, he told the kid. Anything that comes up, you pitch in. Do a good job and you won't regret it. Eddy had no kids of his own and he kind of adopted the tall, skinny kid. Archie was quiet, didn't say much, didn't smile a lot. Shy, kind of. But a thinker. You could almost see the wheels going around in his head when he was sorting things out. Eddy discovered that Archie wrote pretty good and soon had him writing for his direct mail pieces. The response to the mailings went up maybe twenty percent, which meant a lot more profit for Eddy's company. Eddy heaped praise on Archie and rewarded him with a whopping raise. That's the way Eddy was.

"Like the man himself, Eddy's lifestyle was high, wide and handsome. Whatever he did, he went first class. And he was not one of those typical Johnny-come-lately slobs. He was elegant, Eddy was, in his dress and in his manners. He had great taste and could afford to indulge it. His home was a perfect example. Designed by that famous architect, Arthur Emerson. It was right out of *Architectural Digest*. Talk about a show place. All glass and steel and sun decks. An eighteen-bedroom palace with butlers, servants, the whole bit, out on a hill in Caledon. On acres and acres of beautifully landscaped parkland with, as you might expect, an Olympic size swimming pool where he and his wife liked to entertain other big shooters and their wives.

"After Eddy found the pot of gold, he'd also found himself a high society wife. Her name was Emerald. Eddy used to joke that his wife was a gem. Emerald would roll her eyes whenever he did this. Well, what do you expect? She was a Dinsdale. Old money, a humorless bunch, sourpusses, the lot of them, loaded with loot and full of themselves. They felt they were the chosen of god and deserved to be rich.

"Now, Archie Hamill, maybe because his father had been a writer, had hopes of being a writer himself. And since he was, as you might say, an on-the-spot observer of the Palermo story with all its twists and turns, he promised himself that one day he'd write that story. And one day, some years after Eddy's death, he did. And this is it."

After a moment's pause, Professor Whittle puts the manuscript down slowly on the table, looks up, and addresses his class.

"That's where the manuscript ends. It's an unfinished first draft. As I said earlier, Archie couldn't be here today to read this himself. And now that I've read it to you, I want to explain Archie's absence by sharing some very sad news. After the seminar on Friday, while on his way home, Archie was killed by a hit and run driver. In order to be fair to his efforts, I felt I should expose you to his writing before giving you the bad news, so you could consider his work unclouded by the shock of his death. I think we'll all agree that Archie Hamill showed great promise as a writer, and I know we'll all miss him and what I'm sure would have been his thoughtful contributions in our discussions. I've written his mother in Toronto a letter of condolence from all of us. And those of you who would like to can sign it before you leave today. Anybody who prefers to write a letter personally can get Mrs. Hamill's address from me.

SOME DAY, MY PRINCE
Chapter 43

Amazu wasn't just a pretend prince in a bespangled costume. He was a real royal, Crown Prince Amazu, scion of the royal house of Halbin-Somnia. Still, no one paid him much attention, as he strolled, *sans retinue, sans entourage, sans* care, along picturesque Queen Street West, stopping now and then to gaze approvingly into window after window laden with the mo, the po-mo, the no-mo, and, of course, the once-mo, the reusables, the recyclables, the reclaimables, that, having been passed on by their former owners, were now being passed off by wily dealers as collectibles, or even, to the unwary or the unknowledgeable, as antiques. On Queen Street West, after all, one man's junk was another man's junque.

It is fair to say that Amazu had a soft spot for old stuff. His ancestral castle in the province of Tedeum on the upper reaches of the River Vayzmir, in the lower foothills of northwestern Halbin-Somnia was full of it. Halbin-Somnia with its sod huts and sodden outdoor privies was a third world country, or maybe even a fourth, where people still believed in witchcraft and magic and not much else and where causal connections between the sex act and reproduction had yet to be recognized, although they were said to be working on it. To describe the country as backward and awkward might not be appreciated but would not be inappropriate.

Having for the moment, at least, set all that distant and unruly reality aside, Amazu, with his Oxford English, and his unlikely garb, easily passed as a resident of Queen West. Wonky perhaps, offbeat certainly, the slightly grotty neighborhood was notable for its colorful mix of artists, misfits and off-beat characters and their often startlingly individualistic, some might even say, bizarre, modes of attire, as well as their ludicrously loopy hair styles infused, somehow, hair by hair, strand by strand, clump by clump, with wildly strobing fluorescent colors not normally associated with living things, human or otherwise.

It was not surprising then, that in this environment, the Prince's regal attire, the tunic, the sash, the medals, the gold braid, the epaulettes, the tall hat with its ostrich plumes, the saber in its scabbard, the knee-high leather boots, did not so much as raise an eyebrow amongst the local citizenry. Once, in fact, when he removed his hat for a moment to scratch his head, a passerby, taking him for a neighborhood street person, dropped a dollar into it. True, it was a Canadian dollar, a loonie, as it is known, and worth at that time, perhaps only 60 cents in U.S. money. Still, it's the thought that counts, isn't it? Other than that, nobody gave His Royal Fucking Highness a second look. Or even a first.

The accepting environment changed abruptly, however, when the Prince reached the corner of Queen Street and University Avenue, where the Osgoode Hall law courts stood. Here, lawyers in their dark and dismal garb predominated and proliferated. The sidewalks were thick and crawling with them. If the law is an ass, as someone once said, what are we to make of its practitioners? the itinerant Amazu wondered. He made no attempt to answer this question.

At Osgoode Hall Station, fishing about in the innards of his tunic for an elusive subway token, Amazu descended into the subway in the midst of a troop of dark suited, briefcase carrying advocates who shrunk from him, taking great pains to keep their distance from the Halloween left-over, lest the peculiar apparition attempt to engage them in conversation. And when the apparition entered the half-full subway car, all eyes turned in unison to gaze, for a long, lingering moment, in curiosity, if not in amusement, on this most unlikely of fellow travelers. The simultaneity of the stare, this group gawk, so to speak, was accompanied by a momentary hush in the car. Not a word was spoken. Not a snicker heard. Not a sniff. Not a snuffle. Not a smirk. And if, by chance, Amazu looked back into the eyes of any of the lookers, they quickly looked away, averted eyes, blinked, cleared throats, coughed, scratched selves in strange places, played with combination locks on briefcases, or gazed off glassy eyed into space, as if in distant reverie.

Unconcerned by the concerted inspection, Amazu gave it no further thought, found a single seat and clutching his saber in its scabbard close to his side to keep it from rattling, or inadvertently smiting other passengers, he seated himself. When in full regalia, he always chose to sit alone, not out of a desire to avoid contact with commoners but because he found it too crowded to deposit his bulkily adorned wherewithal next to another body. No great hue and cry was raised over this.

The doors closed, as subway doors inevitably do, all eyes turned away, and the train rumbled rapidly southward in the direction of Union Station, where many passengers left the car and a great many more boarded it. In a moment, the seats were all occupied, and the car quickly filled up with standing hangers-on. As the train looped past Union Station, purposefully nosing and noising its way northward, one of the standees, a tall, angular woman in her late thirties, in dark lawyer-like garb – but no briefcase – seized onto the rail above Amazu's seat, planting her considerable and formidable self directly in front of our puzzled prince. Looking weary and woebegone, the woman in black sighed audibly at every jerk of the subway car, glancing, as she did so, at Amazu, who grew increasingly uncomfortable with both the proximity of the woman and what appeared to him to be her distressed behavior.

Finally, when he could bear it no longer, Amazu addressed himself to the cause of his unease. "Are you not well, madam? You appear to be in some distress. Is there something one can do to help?"

Grimacing wearily, the woman leaned in close to him and responded in a whisper. "Something one can do?" she said almost mockingly. "Well, yes. One can give up one's seat to a pregnant woman who feels unwell, if one is so inclined."

Amazu sprang to his well-booted feet. "By all means, madam. Do sit. And accept my apology. I had no idea. Is that better?"

"Yes, thank you." Settled into the seat, she gave him a funny, little smile that he found not at all funny.

A transaction had been completed. They had traded places. Amazu was now holding onto the overhead rail and standing right in front of the pregnant woman, trying not to look down into her face. Finally, he gave up, looked down and in an attempt to be solicitous, asked, "When are you expecting, may I ask?"

"Expecting?" The woman replied, looking annoyed. "Expecting what?"

"Your child. When are you expecting your child?"

"Child? What child?"

"The child you are carrying."

"I'm not carrying a child. I'm not carrying anything, not even a briefcase. Surely you can see that."

Something strange was afoot. Amazu's alarm system sensed it and sounded a terse, early warning, totally devoid of definite articles: "Danger. Danger. Danger. Pursue conversation no further. Move quickly away from woman. Exit car at next stop." But for reasons he would never be able to explain, Amazu clung to the overhead rail and to the conversation.

"But, my dear madam, did you not inform me that you were pregnant?"

"I did and I am. But not with child."

"If not with child, with what, pray, are you pregnant, if I may be so bold?" Amazu persisted.

"With purpose, with possibilities, of course. What else? That should be obvious, surely, to a well- informed prince like yourself."

This took Amazu completely by surprise. "What leads you to assume I am a prince?"

"In that get-up, you're either a prince or a ponce. And you don't strike me as a ponce."

"No, madam. In precisely the same way that you are pregnant but not with child, I am a prince but not."

"How puzzling," said the woman pregnant with purpose and possibilities but not with child. She smiled broadly for the first time. "How very puzzling," said the woman, almost leering at him. "Two puzzled souls in a subway car. Two conundrums to puzzle over. Having traded places, perhaps, we can now trade conundrums, as well."

"To what point?" replied Amazu. "Trading in conundrums is frowned on by my people and forbidden by the constitution of my country. Besides, such trading breaches the bounds of privacy and propriety and is unlikely to confer a benefit on either of us."

The woman sighed ruefully. "I see I've wasted my time on you, prince. Usually, when I seek to acquire a seat with the ploy of pregnancy, I am asked how long I've been pregnant. I'm then able to reply, 'Only fifteen minutes but I'm still tired.' It's an old burlesque joke. But on a crowded subway car, it's usually so embarrassing to the questioner that he goes quickly away. You, unfortunately, sir prince, asked the wrong question, got instead, the puzzling answer, did not go away, and now you refuse to trade conundrums. What shall I do to embarrass you? I know." She rose shakily to her feet. "Here, take your seat back."

Amazu backed away and menacingly put his hand on his saber. "Do not press me, madam. I can be very ugly when crossed."

"You're not frightening me. Besides you're already very ugly."

The train came to a stop at the Rosedale station. Amazu did what he should have done several stops earlier. He turned on his well-booted heel and clutching saber to side, quickly exited the car, rapidly climbed the stairs to the street level, where he stopped to get his bearings.

"Where are you off to, prince?" asked a voice directly behind him. It was the pregnant but not woman in black.

"Are you following me?" asked Amazu accusingly.

"Not really. Rosedale is my stop. I live here." She made no move to leave. "Now that there is no one else about, shall we trade conundrums?"

Amazu looked around. They were alone. He grew quite uneasy. "I would prefer not to, madam."

"Stop calling me, madam," she said staring at him piercingly. "I am not a madam. I am a witch."

"A witch? Which witch?" asked Amazu, sensing what was coming and trying not to evidence his discomfort.

"I, prince, am the witch of which no one is aware. And that is my conundrum. Now, what's yours? Let's have it."

"I did not agree to exchange conundrums with you, madam... er... witch."

"Ah, but now that I've revealed my conundrum to you, prince, you have no choice but to reveal yours to me. I am a witch, after all. And I can compel you to tell."

"No, you cannot. No, you... No, you... Very well, damn you," said the prince who now felt compelled. "I will tell you. But you will pay dearly for this."

"Don't count on it. Well, I'm waiting."

"The fact is, I am not really a prince."

"I might have known," said the witch of which no one is aware."

"What are you then?"

"I am the abandoned offspring of a Viking. I was secretly adopted," Amazu replied, reaching for his saber.

Before he could draw it from its scabbard, the witch said, "Oh, come off it, Your Emptiness. That would be a copycat Viking of a fake Viking. You've been hearing rumors about that long lasting Viking, haven't you? None of that is true, you know. Never aging Viking! Why, that's like believing in fairies. It's fiction for fools like you. All of a sudden, everybody is that fraud's next of kin. Everybody is a Viking. I'm on to you, kiddo. You're no Viking. You're actually – let me see – how about a frog? Yes, that's it. You're actually a frog."

With that, she transfixed him with her wandless, transformational glare and he promptly turned into the frog she had accused him of being and rapidly repaid the witch's efforts by discharging his newly acquired froggy bladder on her recently purchased Nike sneakers. Whereupon the pissed on, pissed-off witch gave the little, freshly minted, green amphibian a swift kick in the slats, sending it tumbling ass over teakettle back down the stairs, onto the subway platform, and out onto the tracks where an oncoming train rolled over it, reducing it to an unprincely green slime with flecks of red.

"Oops," said the witch.

Then, without so much as a glance in the direction of what she had so rottenly wrought, the witch of which no one is aware marched briskly along Roxborough East to her pseudo-baronial townhouse where, after cleaning up her Nikes, she prepared a sumptuous leg of lamb dinner with oven roasted potatoes and carrots for her husband, the busy Chief Executive Officer of a large conglomerate, who was about to come rolling home in his chauffeur-driven Lincoln Town Car after a hectic day in the head office of his company spent in masterfully down-sizing recently acquired high-tech companies, to enjoy a quiet, relaxed evening with his wife, the witch of which no one is aware, including him.

Several months later, in the Halbin-Somnia capital of Cruton, the press, such as it was, the populace and the royal family, each in its own institutionalized way, puzzled over the unexplained disappearance, while on a private visit to Canada, of the royal heir, Crown Prince Amazu. The royal personage had gone missing without a trace. The heir apparent, it was now apparent, was no longer apparent.

And in the Rosedale station, passenger traffic was light, the subway was dark and between the tracks, in those dark spaces, the red flecks persisted.

THE DARK SPACES
Chapter 44

What are we to do about the dark spaces?

Between the tracks,

green slime

and flecks of red.

Flecks of red

you say?

Flecks

of red?

And if the dark spaces aren't worry enough,

what about the ominous silences?

What are we to do about the ominous silences?

And in the intervals, in the slippery, slithery interstices,

between the silences,

what are we to do about the diced voices,

the minced talk,

the finely chopped jabbering.

and the sumptuous

leg of lamb

with flecks

of red?

What are we to do about

the simpering priggishness,

the facelessness,

the gracelessness?

The pissed-on Nikes?

What are we to do?

What are *we* to?

What are …?

But never mind.

Replacements are in place.

Stand-ins are on stand-by.

No bars, no guards,

locked in grubby prisons

of ancient reptilian minds,

shackled are we

to each other

and to yesterday,

to yesteryear.

To yester…

And what of fear?

The fear is near.

It is here.

It does not end. It does not stop.

It just goes on

clippety clop.

What if the universe is just a giant spinning turntable?

And every so often, it suddenly speeds up

and someone randomly flies off into space?

A fleck in space,

red still,

but never heard from

again

UNDERGROUND METAFICTION
Chapter 45

The problem may have been that the antagonist had no photo ID, not even a driver's license with his photo on it. But then, why would he? He didn't drive. He had never driven. He didn't own a car. He had never owned a car. There was no car. And to make matters worse, all four tires were flat. All four. The spare tire may have also been flat. But there was no way to tell, since the spare tire was in the trunk of the car he didn't have, had never had. And who knew where that car was? Or even, if it was. Of course, if it wasn't, this confabulation had the makings of a conundrum. And there is no way on earth that a conundrum with four flat tires can be driven. And what good is a non-drivable conundrum? What's more, conundrums don't, as a rule, park in underground garages, although where they do actually park is uncertain, as well as unlikely. Clearly, this wants explaining.

The non-driver antagonist was trying to explain all this to the tow truck jockey who wasn't really paying attention because he was too busy trying to figure out how to boot his too-high tow truck into the underground garage with the too-steep ramp and the too-low ceiling for his too-high tow truck to navigate. The tow truck driver had been sent to help deal with the dilemma of four flat tires by the motor club that the non-driver hadn't even called since he was not a member. It was all pretty much straightforward and should have been perfectly clear but it made no sense to the tow truck driver who, as noted, really wasn't paying attention but was only interested in how to enter the underground garage so he could deal with the conundrum's four flat tires.

Finally, after a long, silent standstill, the tow truck driver decided he would call off trying to descend into the impossibly configured garage and call the motor club office instead, for a lesser tow truck, a tow truck of lower height. The antagonist tried to dissuade him from doing so but the tow truck driver was adamant and, after calling the motor club office for a replacement tow truck, departed the scene of his parking defeat and a few minutes later, a second tow truck of lower height arrived and was able to descend the steep ramp into the underground garage where there was nothing to be seen, or done, or gained. And the antagonist had to explain to the second tow truck driver, all over again, exactly what was going on, which was not much, if anything.

The antagonist, a professor of English Literature and a longtime literary critic of some note, should have been the ultimate authority and should have had the last word when he described the conundrum as metafiction. The second tow truck driver, however, disagreed. He had a strong sense of self. He was, after all, a dropout from English Literature and had published a poem in a respected literary journal. He insisted that the conundrum was a poem and he refused to be reasoned with. So, the learned professor who was not unsympathetic to struggling young poets, having once been one himself but gotten over it, did not press the matter but let it pass.

ALVARO'S TALE
Chapter 46

Here begins the fretful tale of the nose-to-toes woes of Cuban expatriate, Alvaro Hernandez, former cigar maker and unexpectedly gifted guitar player, transformed, alas, by the direst of circumstances into migrant refugee, after almost losing his life in a frightening misadventure about which you will now be apprised. But first, you are enjoined to acquiesce to this overly early and perhaps irresponsible, interruption in the telling of this tale, this suddenly barging in, so to speak, which may cause a ruckus, in some circles, but perhaps a ruckus is what is warranted to avoid later quibbling and squabbling over what is, or what is not, a proper story as we proceed with this purportedly proper story about Alvaro Hernandez.

For some time before Alvaro Hernandez finally decided he had to leave Havana, his life had been a nightmare. He had said too much, too often, and in all the wrong places and was certain he was being followed, watched, bugged, spied on and increasingly he was feeling threatened. Growing more and more fearful, he made up his anxious mind to escape. Unwisely, he chose to do so in the company of six other desperate souls in a leaky, overloaded, rubber dinghy that swamped and went down in heavy seas, in the Straits of Florida, and sad to say, took the lives of all six of his unfortunate fellow travelers.

Miraculously, Alvaro did not drown but was saved by a child's inflatable toy, a duck-shaped polyvinyl chloride floater, still in its package left behind in one of the dinghy's storage pockets by some previous voyager. The PVC duck, designed to automatically inflate when wet, kept Alvaro afloat, albeit only barely, but at least with his head out of the water, until, drifting in and out of consciousness and verging on hypothermia, he was fished out of the sea like a tarpon by the U.S. Coast Guard and taken to the base hospital at the Coast Guard station in Fort Lauderdale on the Florida mainland where, foot cuffed to the bed, illegal migrant style, he slowly recovered and his miraculously saved life went on, though things didn't get any better. They got worse.

Stop! Here is what you should know, before you go any further. No matter what you may think, based on your previous reading, this story is not a tale unto itself. It is an integral part of a novel, which by design, or lack of it, or by inadvertence, is not necessarily in chronological order. Granted, these days, order of any kind, including chronological, is not the be-all and end-all of nervy, topsy-turvy novels like this one. A more troublesome concern could well be this novel's lack of logic. But then again, how much logic is around in these troubled times? Take breaking news, for example. Is it any wonder it's breaking? The fact is, it's a zoo out there. As unlikely as it is, there may be the odd tiger prowling around, but let's get serious, mostly, it's apes, devious apes. And that's on weekdays. On weekends, it's Dante's Inferno, and more apes, scheming simians, from whom we've evolved to be what we are, which augmented with a question mark is a good question.

The year before Alvaro's near demise by drowning had not been a good one for the once upon a cigar maker. Cigar smoking had fallen from fashion and slipped in sales. Cigar making as a craft had tumbled off a cliff and taken Alvaro's income down and out with it. To make matters worse, two months before his disastrous, near-death, maritime experience, his wife, Hermosa, was overcome by a mysterious, undiagnosed but deadly ailment and had died in the ambulance on her way to the renowned Calixto García Hospital Emergency Room in Havana. Ironically, *The Lancet*, the weekly, peer-reviewed publication, one of the oldest and best known independent, international general medical journals, hails it as among the best medical facilities in the world. And without question, it is. But of course, to access its benefits, you have to be there and to be there, you have to first get there. Life is not simple. It can kill you.

Alvaro was devastated by Hermosa's death. Alvaro and Hermosa had, sad to say, been childless. Hermosa had suffered several miscarriages and never gone full term. There were no children to grieve or mourn or bolster the lone survivor. It was an unhappy time. And a lonely one.

In any event, and there are many in this tale that are likely to be ontological or metaphysical, which, if the terminology doesn't intimidate you, may sound impressive and appear to promise a good read but can, nonetheless, be endlessly perplexing about what this novel purports to be, but may, or may not be, which is to say, fiction.

This raises a question about this fiction, so called, and its perpetrator. In the light of his own, off-the-wall curriculum vitae, *is it possible, doubters may wonder, if this is all not merely a fiction but a flimflam, the work of some peripatetic, 1300-year-old Viking warrior/poet and obsessive scrivener, hiding behind many, many authors, many, many times, in many, many places, who may be trying to slyly pass off his own actual, albeit highly unlikely, reality as fiction? If so, the disbelievers say, he will only succeed in doing so, if readers like you permit it. Will you permit it? Or will you join the disputers and resist and insist on being told a story, a proper story, so called, beginning, middle, end, like this one about Alvaro Hernandez? At least to begin with. But to resume.*

Alvaro had chosen Regina, Saskatchewan, an unlikely destination only because of Hermosa's nephew, Paz, who taught Latin American studies at Regina College, a branch campus of the University of Saskatchewan, and had promised to help Alvaro get settled and find a job. But Alvaro's route to Regina had turned out to be an obstacle course, long, arduous and after his recovery from near drowning, delayed by U.S. Immigration and a deportation order in Miami, followed by detention for a month in a caged lockup for illegal migrants before being abruptly released without explanation and helicoptered sneakily out to almost nowhere in North Dakota and then dropped off in a farmer's field near the unguarded Canadian border from which he had to walk in torn shoes across snow-covered fields the rest of the way into Canada. Oh Canada.

Further complicating Alvaro's seemingly unending misadventure, Paz, while waiting for the much-delayed Alvaro to arrive, had unexpectedly been recruited for a diplomatic posting in Barcelona that included a government provided residence and a teaching job for his teacher/wife, Mariana. It was a once in a lifetime opportunity, as careers go, for both of them and far too good to turn down, and so Paz and Mariana accepted and were preparing to move on to Barcelona, while at the same time Paz was trying to get Alvaro settled and organized as best he could. It was complicated.

Now, six months later, with Paz and Mariana off in Barcelona, Alvaro still had no English to speak of, no job to earn and learn from and no prospects to have high hopes for. Paz had found him a bare bones basement rental apartment and set him up with a bank account and a little money, but the money soon ran out.

A devastating hurricane brought terrifying winds and torrents of rain and flooding and wide power outages, followed by hail the size of golf balls, destroying the little left of Saskatchewan's crops, wiping out food supplies and demolishing the food banks which in any case had run out. Drought and famine took over what was left of the land, on which starving scavengers roamed, living out of garbage cans when they could.

Everything that could possibly go wrong, went wrong. And continued to go wrong. And when it was thought to be over and done with, it wasn't either of those. There was more flooding, more anguish. Alvaro had always doubted the existence of god but was on the fence. He wasn't certain. Now, he was certain.

There was rot and mold everywhere, and no food anywhere. The ceiling of the rental leaked. The walls reeked. The ancient, rusted window fan squeaked and squealed and squawked until it slowly choked itself off and died a noisy, rattling death. Unbelievably, the heat in Regina was worse than in Havana and more unbearable. The rent had not been paid for three months and the landlord, a numbered company, in the Cayman Islands, specializing in anonymous tax avoidance, did not respond to complaints, did no repairs and was threatening tenants with eviction. There were unpaid repair bills piled up on the kitchen table for unfinished work but no money or insurance coverage to pay for them and a shoebox full of medical bills for which Alvaro was not covered since, as a new resident, he was not yet registered and not eligible for the provincial health plan.

Paz did his best to help from afar but when Mariana gave birth to their first child, who was born with special needs, she had no option but to give up her teaching job and suddenly they were a one salary family, and the cash flow was reduced not only for them but also in their aid for Alvaro.

Alvaro grew increasingly desperate. He had to do something. But what? His once well-paying expertise as a cigar maker had become valueless. Cigar making was a no-go. Cigar usage had diminished to little more than a prop in second-rate movies.

There were two carwashes in Regina, where there was usually minimum wage work for migrants who could find work nowhere else. But Regina was experiencing a post-hurricane, post flooding drought, and water usage was restricted, and the car washes were forced to close.

Alvaro cast about for a solution to his predicament. He had played guitar back in Havana and had a large repertoire of Latin American songs. It occurred to him that perhaps he could make a little money busking on the street, but he had lost his guitar in the treacherous ocean crossing when the dinghy had gone down. He had neither a guitar to play, nor money to pay for one.

He considered semi-seriously, after much agonizing, that maybe the only thing to do was to rob a bank to get enough money to buy a guitar. It would be a one-time thing. He was not about to become a career bank robber. He began to make a plan to work out how to go about this unwise project.

First of all, he would not attempt to rob his own bank. He was known and would be recognized. It was too risky. Secondly, he didn't have a gun and could not afford to buy one, even if he knew where to do so. He would have to commit the robbery with no weapon to threaten bank tellers. And thirdly, any threat to bank employees would have to be verbal. How would that work? How would he persuade them to cooperate? What would he say? How could he verbally intimidate bank employees when he had no language to do so, no English? Would he have to bring a translator with him as an accomplice? It was not only fool-hardy but ludicrous, he realized. He quickly abandoned the bank robbery idea. He needed another scheme.

There were three music stores in Regina, all in one block on Albert Street, and Alvaro prowled their aisles frequently, silently looking at acoustic guitars knowing he was unable to buy but hoping for a miracle of some kind but not really expecting one.

The unexpected miracle turned out to be a teenaged student who played guitar and clerked in the music store after class. His name tag said Diego. And miracle of miracles, Diego was the child of immigrants from Costa Rica and spoke Spanish. Alvaro could not believe his good luck. He could have a conversation.

"Would you like to try out one of the guitars, *señor*?"

"I am a refugee and out of work and have no money. I cannot afford to buy."

"Still," said Diego, "you can afford to try. It costs nothing to try. And maybe your fortunes will change, and you will be able to afford to buy later. I play guitar myself. Let me help you. Which one would you like to try?"

"Perhaps the Martin Smith?"

"Good. Would you like me to tune it for you?"

"That will not be necessary. I can do it."

Alvaro adjusted the tuning pegs on the guitar, plucked some strings, playfully, strummed a few chords, smiled, and then, closing his eyes, played with purpose and in a clear and haunting tenor voice sang plaintively in Spanish, of life and death, of love and loss, of hope and home. The busy store, staff and customers, all, went awesomely silent, listening and marveling. It was a magic moment, followed by applause from everybody in the store.

Well now! Isn't that good news! Alvaro's troubles certainly seem to have ended. Happy endings to the story are bubbling up all over in the writer's mind. Which one will it be? Will Alvaro be saved by music? Maybe he gets a recording contract and becomes a hit worldwide? Or maybe he returns to Cuba where they name a music theater after him and establish a National Alvaro day. Or the PVC duck that saved his life is recreated as the giant centerpiece of a fountain in a park that bears Alvaro's name. Or maybe a movie is made of his life starring a younger and even handsomer Javier Bardem type. Oh, all the happy little endings are lining up like chicks for their turn to fly or whatever it is the chicks do.

But maybe it doesn't work out that way at all. Maybe Alvaro's life takes a downturn. He gets into drugs. Or a destructive relationship ruins his budding career. Or maybe the novel turns out to be not a novel after all, but merely a short story, a very short story, where Alvaro is murdered on page ten in a dark alley for his first-earned hundred bucks.

But that's the writer's dilemma, isn't it? Anything could happen now. ANYTHING! Anything at all that the writer can dream up. And only the writer knows which anything will get his nod, except, in this case, he doesn't. Not this writer, anyway. And that's not the only problem. Happy endings don't really interest him anymore, and he feels strongly that Alvaro has already had his share of shit.

So, let's just turn the lights out now, shall we?

INFINITY TAKES TOO LONG
Chapter 47

Despite the repeated insistence of cutting edge, over the top, state of the art technology, Infinity is not just around the corner. The disquieting thing is that there is no corner. Infinity, like it or not, take it or leave it, is not around the corner. It's not around. Period.

The long and short of it, or maybe it's the long and longer of it, the problem with Infinity is that it takes too long, way, way, too long. But then, a series of unsettling questions arises: What's wrong with too long? Why is too long a problem? What's the bloody rush? Who among us is lined up, waiting or wanting, to be Infinite or simply to get to Infinity? And here comes the big one. If waiting on Infinity is a problem, whose problem is it, anyway?

On the other hand, what if Infinity is not the problem? What if, despite all the tiresome mouthing off and bleating blabber, no one really cares about Infinity? You hear about Doctors of Divinity all the time. There's one sermonizing away at you at every turn, on almost every corner but you never hear of Doctors of Infinity, or PhDs in Infinity, or Infinitologists, or Infinity specialists, or Infinity consultants. There are no Infinity courses in the schools, colleges or universities. Or even on YouTube. Planes, trains, buses, none of them go to Infinity. Even Uber doesn't go there. What good is Infinity, if you can't go there, can't get there?

Who feels shortchanged when it comes to Infinity? Let's have a show of hands. No hands. Let's have a list of names. No names. You see? Infinity has no friends. If you were fundraising for Infinity, the coffers would be empty.

Time, too, is without friends. It shares that fate with its close relative, Infinity. Nevertheless, we're tethered to Time. Or chained. How about entrapped? Entrapped by Time. That works at least till Time runs out and then you're not only free, you're out of Time and out of luck.

And when did Time begin? What if it turns out there was no beginning? What if there was no bang, big or small? What if it all began with just a little whimper? What if the beginning is so far back in Time that it has been forgotten, lost, stolen? Or revolving in space beyond our reach, or ken, or marinating in cold-pressed extra virgin olive oil from Andalucía? Time seems to go on forever but how long is that? On, and on, and on, all the way to Infinity? And why does it matter if you can't either get there or be there? And here's the most agonizing problem, what if there's no "you" left when you get there?

Time always takes its toll. There's no getting away from it. Cells can't go on forever or even for a seriously long while. Each cell is a life, an existence unto itself. It has limits. Cells wear out and cell death is inevitable. Cell walls collapse and buckle and burst and nuclei escape and then it's cell out and cell over and game's up.

The car analogy might help. Don't be fooled by the paint job. Under the hood, the parts are going. Luckily for us, this is the era of parts replacement, and though there are many more of us, many more of the many more are now being kept going by implanted devices. Far, far, far, in the future, when bodies in graveyards have turned to dust, those graveyards will become repositories of ancient, once life-extending digital components and electronic implants and miscellaneous hardware. They will be high tech dumps. They may even buzz or light up at night. Or send signals to Infinity.

Sounds like great times ahead.

PART THREE
Endgames

ENDGAME: As Tragedy
Chapter 48

It's a brisk autumn day in Bellwoods Park. The sun, low in the late afternoon sky, shines a sharp shaft of light on two men sitting on a bench under an ancient oak tree, said to be 800 years old. Suddenly, a capricious gust of wind disturbs the autumn leaves clinging precariously to the branches of the old oak, setting them adrift, a few at a time. One of the benchers, the one in a suit jacket, blue shirt, no tie, brushes fallen leaves from his shoulders, and turns to his companion. "Looks like we're winding down, Thorsten. Or winding up. Odd, isn't it, that both mean the same thing, namely goodbye?"

There is no response from his companion, so a few moments later he tries again: "Is this goodbye, then?"

"I don't do goodbyes. Have you forgotten?"

"No, of course not. You never say goodbye. Without a word, without so much as a fare-thee-well, you just up and run."

This pointed-stick-in-the-eye reply elicits a small, tight smile and more silence from his bench-mate who sits clutching a large burlap bag tied with leather thongs, and who, in concert with the pause in the conversation, looks away to marvel at how many people in the park had dogs.

Dogs. He'd once had a dog, he recalls. His name was Presto. Beautiful Presto. Ahh, and he'd also had another dog called

Thunder! I've had two dogs! He marvels again, doggedly, at his own long, remarkable history. Two dogs. Who would believe it? He can scarcely believe it himself, says nothing, remains silent, pensive, almost, but not sentimental. That's not what 1300-year-old Vikings do. They sulk.

The sun, sinking more quickly now, teeter-totters precariously on the rooftops of the buildings along Queen Street West, looking as though it was about to tumble off and roll down the street, a giant orange bowling ball burning everything in its fiery path.

The other bench-sitter, the one in the suit jacket, blue shirt, no tie, tries again: "I see you're carrying your gear, Thorsten," he says, tilting his head in the direction of the burlap bag. "So... just to, sort of, wrap up, I thought we could maybe talk about a few things."

Still focused on the park's canine activity, the man with the burlap bag answers distractedly, "Fine." Then, turning to his companion with sudden renewed interest, "By the way, August. Where's Satch? I haven't seen Satchimotomonkeyman in a little while."

"Thorsten, you haven't seen him in a *long* while. Thanks for noticing. Finally."

"Why are you being so prickly, August? I just asked a simple question about your dog. Where is he these days?"

"I'd have thought that you, as the author, would be the first to know. Satch is living in Belgrade now.

"Why Belgrade? What's he doing there?"

"After you displaced us, and Satch lost his column at the *Post*, he was writing a newsletter from Aunt Polly's, and scratching around to find work. Then, he got an overseas job offer and went to Serbia to cover the making of a film being shot by four men on horseback, so it was quite a challenge for Satch. He had to learn to ride, which he did with ease, apparently, and the Serbs were so impressed with his incredible skills, they convinced him to stay there and write his Dog Log column for the *Belgrade Daily News*. He's become quite famous. He still finds the time to write to me, though. Now and then."

"In English or Serbian?"

"A bit of both. He was always a quick learner."

"Nice story, August. Maybe I'll write about it."

"Well, I would rather you write him a plane ticket to come home, if you don't mind. I miss him and I'm sure Natalie does, too."

"Ahh, yes, Natalie! She still making her signature lasagna? "

"Not as far as I know. I don't even know where she is now. She could still be sitting at the kitchen table at Aunt Polly's for all I know, telling me to answer the phone."

"Don't be ridiculous, August. No one can sit in one place for a whole book. Besides, you did answer the phone, or we wouldn't be sitting here together right now, in this noisy park, on this hard bench, and under this woebegone and endlessly shedding tree."

"But where is she? You haven't ever, in this whole book, said where Natalie is. You've hardly even mentioned her."

"There you go again, August. Blaming me. Why is everything always up to me?"

"I won't even to try to answer that, Thorsten. But you're the author, so, you know, just kind of think about it."

Just then, a little girl about ten years old, in a Girl Guide uniform, approaches Thorsten, and with an eager tilt of her head, asks him, "Would you like to buy some Girl Guide cookies, Mister?"

Thorsten reaches into his pocket and comes out with a ten-dollar bill, "Here you go. Is this enough?"

"Yes, umm, I mean no, I mean – it's too much, sir…" she starts to say.

"Go ahead, take it and … and get yourself a coffee. Bye bye now."

The two men fall silent as the falling leaves swirl around them. "Where is Erland and his magic when you need him?" thinks Thorsten as he brushes off his shoulder and turns to his companion.

"Before we are both buried by these ill-fated leaves, August, what is it you wanted to talk about?"

"Well, for starters, maybe you wouldn't mind telling me what happened to the novel that you were in the middle of writing."

"Ah, yes. The novel. Okay, what about it? "

'Well, there you were, deep in the mystery of Giggle, with Rampa, and Althea, and the scooper, and Stretch, and I was there doing my detective job, then everything just stopped. You went into seclusion."

"Not simply seclusion, August! I was working." Thorsten takes a deep breath and seems to be gathering his thoughts before continuing. "Pity the poor author, August, if, in exultant *media res*, something he has just written, something that just slipped, or dripped, from his pen, sparks a new thought and sends his imagination careening off track in another direction."

"Could you be a little more specific?"

"Sure. Here's what happened. When I started to write *Return of The Secret Viking*, it seemed to me that using a search engine that I would call Giggle to help you find me would provide enough plot possibilities to create a contemporary, find-the-needle-in-a haystack story in which I, once again, would be the needle to be found. The book was to be a recognizable sequel to *The Secret Viking*, but with a different motivation for the chase. You, Professor August Dallou, would have a temper tantrum up front in which you reclaimed your existence and your right to have a role in this sequel. That would cast the book as a kind of revenge tale, with you the hopping mad, angry adversary this time, not the noble 'bring knowledge to the world' pilgrim of the first book. You would have more of a personal stake in this story. Nice switch, I thought. It felt like an idea that I could develop humorously, absurdly, ironically, and at first, I was exhilarated by all the possibilities. I began all-out to explore that idea. I was all gung-ho!"

"Okay, so you were all gung-ho, but … then what happened?"

"It didn't take long for me to realize I didn't want to write another story where you chase me around the world, even if you were going to use that eccentric, and if I may say, ingenious, search engine I invented to help you do it. I asked myself since you had found me once, would there be any reason for you to find me again? Not really. There was no reason. So, I contacted you, right up front in the book, and enlisted your services not simply as a sleuth trying to track me down again, but as both a character in the book and a consultant to me, the author. I phoned you to come back into the book and help me find a new direction. I phoned you! Don't you remember?"

"Of course, I remember. The phone call came in the middle of Aunt Polly's scrambled eggs."

"And at first it went quite well, didn't it? You and me? You got to work right away. You immediately became suspicious of the whole Giggle set-up including Althea and that blasted buffet of theirs. You sensed that Lion would go to any lengths, treacherous lengths, to convince me to join Reductio, so I decided to go with that as the story for the novel. You were the one who put this train on track, August. It all started the day you came back on the job."

"Well, that's all very flattering, I suppose. But now look at us. Look where we are. The train has stalled, gone completely off track."

"Or maybe it found another way to reach its destination, August. It switched tracks. Trains do that, you know."

"Fine. But why did you keep the same old freight cars sitting there going nowhere, with the Giggles, the mysterious phone calls, the Lions, the steely-eyed, cold-blooded assassins? Where,

I ask you, is all that now? Where did it go? What's been happening while you've been off writing those stories of yours, about a Cessna that won't fly, and a car that won't start, and a prince who turns into a frog, and who knows what else. Thorsten, can you explain what you're doing?"

"Well, in retrospect, I guess I'd written myself into a corner and just didn't know what to do with what I'd started. Waiting on inspiration to strike, I began to explore these stories. My hope was that the stories would reveal the evolution of this work, expose the *pentimenti*, acknowledge the *memento mori* and dig deep holes to see what climbs out."

"Oh c'mon, Thorsten! You were writing a novel, and now it's all fallen apart. What did those stories have to do with the novel?"

"Everything, I hope. I believe they were quite in keeping with what I had started. In fact, they may all be telling the same story, but with different characters. Don't you see, August? The one constant idea is that *everything* is falling apart. The stories deal with that in their own way."

"Maybe they do. But they aren't, and they can't be, a substitute for the main event. Readers will still want to know what happened in the *actual* plot of the *actual* novel you started. Tell us what happened to the Giggle threat to your life. Tell us more about the machinations of Lion and the rest of his henchmen. What does Stretch do, and what becomes of him? I think you should play fair, that's all."

"All right, all right. I get it. So, let's see. You think I should have dealt with ... with what? The kidnapping threat?"

"Well, yes. That might have been a good place to start. "

"Okay. So, I get kidnapped. Let's think about that. Hmmm, let me see…"

Dallou took a deep breath and moved on cautiously. "We don't need to think about that."

"We don't? How so?"

"It's too late."

"What do you mean, too late?"

"It's already happened."

"What on earth are you talking about, August? Look at me. I'm right here. Nobody kidnapped me."

"I guess you haven't been reading the papers."

"Will you please explain what you're talking about? Do I look like I've been kidnapped?"

"Thorsten, we suspected from the very beginning that if Lion failed to negotiate you into joining Reductio, he was going to try and kidnap you and force you into joining them. So, that's what happened. That's all."

"Wait a minute. You're saying Lion kidnapped me?"

"No, not Lion himself. He had Stretch do it. Or rather *not* do it. But he *tried* to."

"This is ridiculous, August. Was I hurt?"

"You weren't hurt. You weren't even there. Here's the story.

Bjorn Igor Svarez, the famous tennis pro, was in town to support a youth tennis program and help raise money for disadvantaged kids to play tennis. The organizers rented the house across from Casa Loma, where you had been living, for Bjorn to stay in for the week that he was here in Toronto. Do you see where I'm going with this, Thorsten?"

"So … Stretch went to my old place?"

"Exactly. He pulled up to the front door of that house in the black limo. He and his driver, also a big guy, sort of a 'heavy,' got out and Stretch rang the doorbell. It was the middle of the night, so he had to push the buzzer several times, and finally Bjorn, in his jockeys, half asleep, red-eyed and orange beard all askew, came to the door. Stretch swiftly pounced on the guy and plastered a cloth loaded with chloroform smack on Bjorn's face. Bjorn went down and Stretch and the limo driver started to carry him to the limo which was parked and waiting on the street. But as they got to the sidewalk where that streetlight that you always complained was shining in your bedroom window stood, and the light clearly illuminated their captive's face, Stretch saw that it was not you. They dropped Bjorn like a hot potato right there on the sidewalk and took off."

"And all this was on the news? How can that be? I didn't write that! It never happened!"

"No, you didn't write it. But it did happen."

"Well, who… who…? Wait a minute, August… did… did you…?"

"Yes, I did." Dallou was smiling from ear to ear. "Do you like it?"

"Do I like it? Why would I like it? I can't believe this! You've stolen my voice! Bloody hell, August!"

"Don't get upset, Thorsten. Have you forgotten? You told me to use my… I believe you called it my 'incredible ingenuity' as a character in this novel… to make the plot work. 'It's what characters in novels do,' you said. 'Just go and make something happen. Do your job, August,' you told me. So that's what I did."

"Good god!"

"I'm sorry if I stepped on your toes. Being a character in a novel is not just a walk in the park, you know. There are heavy responsibilities."

"What have I done? I've created a monster!"

"Settle down, Thorsten, please. The point is not whether I'm a monster or not, although I prefer not to think of myself in that way. The point is, are you happy with what I've written, or not? It was an attempt to help you out. But if you don't like it, you can do it over. It's just words on paper. Nobody suffered. No one was even hurt. Do it your way. Do it any way you like. But do it, damnit! You agreed with me that if Lion's attempt to negotiate your joining up with Reductio were to fail, a kidnapping would be the next step, so either it has to happen, or the reader needs to know why not! And there you were, busy writing about some drowning guy who is saved by a PVC duckie or something."

The air between the two men was once again heavy and laden

with dark clouds. But lightning didn't strike, at least not immediately.

Thorsten finally broke the silence. "It wasn't a 'duckie.' It was a
duck. Just a duck. Stop calling it a 'duckie.'"

The after-work dog-walkers in Bellwoods Park were a garrulous
bunch, and as they strolled past on the nearby path, their conversations drifted into audibility and, moments later, out again into
silence. They came, they went, they paused, they passed on by.
And from the tennis court over to the right of the bench, the noisy
binks and bonks of a little yellow tennis ball being slammed
back and forth across a ragged net slung crookedly between two
sweaty, overweight players wielding rickety racquets and grunt-
ing with every slam punctuated the shrill laughter of children
in the playground, squealing in delight as their swings swung
up, then growing silent on the backward swoop, catching their
breath for the next swing up and the opportunity to squeal again.
Others were descending the slide, climbing back up and descending again. All seemed to be enjoying themselves except for an
unhappy pair of probably four-year-olds in the sand box arguing
to the point of tears over a red dump truck that seemed somehow
to belong to both and to neither at the same time depending on
which of the two was hollering the loudest.

And Dallou wasn't about to let go of his argument either. "The
fact is, say what you will, this book is not a finished work by a
long shot, Thorsten. We do not have the whole enchilada here,"
he protested. "Lion's attempted negotiations failed. Then the
kidnap attempt failed. So now we need to know what Lion is
going to do next. With two attempts to take you on board now
tried and failed, I think the scene could turn downright danger-

ous for you. Lion is not the type of guy who's simply going to fade to black. His show is not over. We need to know what happens. You need to tell us."

"I'm having trouble hearing you. Speak up, August. It's very noisy out here in our office today."

"I'm asking about Lion. What will he do next? You gave him a good backstory and build up, he seemed like a strong character, a vexatious villain. We even knew where he was born and where he went to school, or rather didn't go to school, but we don't know where he is now, or what his plan is."

"Well, let me think about it... okay, well... how about this? Let's say Lion does get on that plane to Paris that I mentioned earlier. Let's say he's going there to officiate at *La Grande Ouverture Officielle* of the newer, bigger, better Giggle. The French were going to name their version of the mighty colossus *Le Gloussement*, but since the meaning of *'gloussement'* is closer to the English 'cackle' or 'cluck' than 'giggle,' they stayed with Giggle. The mighty search engine's new presence in Paris is an international event and the media are full of it: 'GIGGLE GOES TO PARIS.' But the plane that Lion is on, doesn't go to Paris. Let's say it goes down in the Atlantic instead. And then Lion not only sleeps with the fishes, but moments later gets eaten by a shark."

"The plane goes down? With all those people on board?"

"No, no, no. Nothing like that. It wouldn't be a major airline. Let's say it would be a Giggle-owned, business jet."

"Who's the pilot? Who else is on the plane?"

"Althea could be the pilot. Turns out that when she wasn't on

237

Giggle duty, she took some flying lessons and had gotten herself certified to fly jets. And, just to keep it all neat and tidy, the scooper should be on that doomed plane along with Lion and Althea since they're all connected to Giggle. And so they all go down for a bath. And with the entire management team gone, lost for good and out of the picture, Reductio International also fizzles and folds. Then, like the last piece in a game of dominoes, Giggle fails and falls. It fails and falls in Toronto, it fails and falls in Paris, and it fails and falls in the Halbin-Somnia capital of Cruton. And then the game's up. How's that for a scenario, August?"

"Hold on. So, everybody goes down at once? That's a little too convenient, don't you think, Thorsten? And maybe a tad severe?" Dallou adds. "Here's another idea. What do you think of this: How about you bring the Giggle inventor, Casimir Smirkovsky, back into the story? Say he comes to the big Giggle opening in Paris, along with his Swiss banker of course, who still refuses to be identified by name, but that doesn't matter because he brings all the money. They hook up with Lion *et al*, and together they run Reductio International through Giggle, which would reclaim one of its original names, Giggle:Smirk, to acknowledge the return to the fold of its inventor. With this new infusion of money from Smirkovsky, along with its European presence in Paris, Giggle is now so powerful and influential that Lion and his Reductio International no longer need your participation, Thorsten. The plot to get you on board with them gets pushed aside, forgotten, sidetracked, mothballed, put on a back shelf somewhere, hung out to dry. Lion forgets about you."

"He forgets about me?"

"Yes. They don't need you anymore. You're no longer on his radar."

"Interesting, August. Interesting. And, if I may say, not just a little hurtful. It's not my usual style to write myself off and out of the picture like that. But there's another problem with this scenario of yours as well. It doesn't lead to an ending. It's more like the beginning of another book, let's call it 'REDUCTIO RISING' or 'GIGGLE: THE ROSY FINGER OF DAWN.' But it's interesting that you've come up with this idea, August, because it sheds light on something that I, too, am always facing as a writer. And clearly, it's precisely what I'm facing right now and what you're criticizing me for. And you're right, I am avoiding coming to an ending for this novel. The truth is, I'm morbidly uncomfortable with the concept of endings in general. Death is an ending, and by definition or by implicit contractual arrangement is, sad to say, so finite, so finished, so final, that it boggles, although there may not be much left to boggle at that point. Endings shut us down, turn us off, trip us up, remind us that we're frail, fragile, finite, running out of time, out of gas, out of the living breath of life itself. And then the inevitable happens and bye-bye, the party's over. And if we're talking about party as a metaphor for life, it doesn't matter how careful you are driving home, you're not going to get there."

Dallou determinately shakes his head. "When I last checked though, providing some kind of ending to the story was one of the jobs of the author."

"Hold it there, August. I still maintain the story is whatever the author makes of it as he writes it. That story can change, switch direction, dig deeper, fly higher, go off course, change track, you name it, with every word the author writes, wherever his typing fingers take him, the story shifts, it changes, it veers, it digs its own deep holes to climb into or out of."

"So, you've said before. Well, this one hasn't climbed out of its hole yet."

"Wait a minute, who can say if the whole story has been told or not? Maybe there is no whole story. And besides, what's all this fuss about the story anyway? If a book is all story and nothing more, you might as well watch the evening news instead and go to bed."

"I'm sorry, Thorsten, I see you're upset. But there's no getting away from it, stories have a shape, and that includes coming to an end. Readers expect that."

"Well let's say that for now, at least, this story is what it is. Take it or leave it. It's finished and done."

The man in the jacket, blue shirt, no tie, was shivering now that the sun had abandoned the sky. The silence that hung between the two men was long, heavy and loaded. But August Dallou had one more question.

"And me, Thorsten? Where do I stand? Am I being written off and out too? Or do I just sit on this bench forever and, as you say, get buried in the leaves of our office that is no longer our office?"

"August, you haven't heard a word I've said. You never listen to me. How could you not know, how could you *possibly* not know, that you are my heart and soul? All the ants at this bloody picnic know I do not have my own of either of those things. I carry you with me wherever I go. You are always in my mind.

240

We may disagree at times, but that's life. I do listen to you. Intermittently."

"I hear you. Intermittently."

"Dammit, August, no. No, I have not written you off. Not by a long shot. There's your answer."

The sun had fallen into the pit of the horizon and the blue glow of magic hour seeped into Queen Street West and Bellwoods Park. The dog-walkers and their dogs were trotting off home to dinner and din-din, the binkers and bonkers had won and lost and left, and the little yellow tennis ball that had been hit over the top of the chain link fence that surrounded the tennis courts had landed in the tall grass below and was found by Nola, a fine-looking Kerry Blue, who took it home and hid it in the front hall closet with the rest of her collection. The children were dragged home to a supper they probably wouldn't eat because there was too much broccoli on the plate again, and one by one, the lights came on in the row of shops across the street from the bench that sits under the oak tree that had shed its final leaf on the Viking's shoulder.

Thorsten rises from the bench and points across the street, "Look over there, August. See that bookstore?"

"Type Books. Good name for a bookstore. What about it?"

"There's a book launch poster in the window. What does it say?"

"Meet the author."

"Read the book title. "

"*Return of The Secret Viking*." Dallou turns to his bench mate,

"Wait a minute, Thorsten. Haven't we had this conversation before?"

"Right! But that was many pages ago, and everything has changed since then. Back then I told you that you were – to put it a bit harshly, perhaps – that you were simply a character in my book, and that I was the writer."

"Remind me, was that your 'the writer is god' speech?"

"No, I don't think so. You're getting them mixed up. Anyway, it turns out those jobs got a little intermingled this time. Writers are characters, characters are writers. So enough. No more arguments. Okay? Let's go across the street and visit our book. I'll bet there's a pretty large crowd in there. Come on, August, this is our chance to surprise a few people."

Meanwhile, behind the bench, farther back in the park and just beyond the tennis courts, a particularly tall man crouches furtively behind a clump of evergreens as he meticulously assembles a sniper's rifle from the components in his backpack, carefully clicking all the necessary parts into precise places. When that is done, he takes a single bullet from its case and loads into the chamber of the rifle. And then, with visions of the big payout dancing like sugarplums in his head, the former little Sidney Wilks of Mount Airy, West Virginia, who now greatly prefers the name Stretch, stands tall and focused in his black suit and Wall street tie, ready to fulfill his deadly assignment.

But just then, at that very moment, a little girl, about ten years old, wearing a Girl Guide uniform, approaches, hoping to find one last customer on her fundraising mission. She stops to ask the man, "Would you like to buy some cookies, Mister?"

Quickly yanking the rifle behind his back, he hisses at her, "Shoo! Shoo! Go away!"

The earnest little Girl Guide stands frozen in place, stunned at the response.

"Get out of here," the rifleman snarls, "Get lost!"

"What a meanie. So rude," thinks the little girl as she stomps off.

In the distance, in the fast-fading light, and just beyond the tennis courts, a little over from the sandbox and the kiddie swings, and slightly off to one side of the old oak, a solitary figure rises from the bench and gestures in the direction of the bookstore across the street. The sniper, taking this as his cue, steps out silently and swiftly from behind the evergreens, raises the rifle to his shoulder, takes careful aim, and pulls the trigger. Bingo!

Down the Viking goes. Down, slowly, ever so slowly, down, down he goes. Twisting as he's falling, slowly falling, falling and twisting down into the grass and the gravel and the fallen leaves. Down, down he goes, twisting down, falling through the days, the years, the centuries, through the leaves and the lives he had lived, through the books, all the books, he had written, down he goes, down, downward into darkness. Out of light, out of time, out of gas, out of the living breath of life itself, as he would have put it.

Emergency crews are called, but it's too late. Centuries, thirteen centuries, 1300 candles on that mighty cake now instantly extinguished with a single blast from a sniper's full hardware package.

The Viking is no more.

[solemn silence]

"So, you actually spoke to this man earlier in the day?" the policeman asks the earnest little Girl Guide, "And he bought some cookies from you?"

"Yes. He was a nice man."

"Was anyone with him?"

"No. No one was with him. He was alone. But he was kind of talking to himself." she answered. "I felt sorry for him."

The following day, a notice on the second page of the *Toronto Star* reported: "Homeless Man Shot Dead in Bellwoods Park." The article went on to say the assassinated man had worn a kilt and knee sox, and the burlap bag he carried contained ancient Norse artifacts. No one laid claim to the artifacts, and later the Norse Museum in Oslo was grateful to receive them as a gift from the city of Toronto. The kilt found its way to a Salvation Army store where it languishes still.

The shooter, Sydney Wilks of Mount Airy, West Virginia, U.S.A., who answered to Stretch, which he much preferred, was later arrested and charged when he tried to collect one million U.S. dollars from Lion Rampa, the leader of the newly established political party, Reductio International. But Mr. Rampa had died earlier that same day when his plane mysteriously went down in the Atlantic on a flight to Paris. When Mr. Wilks attempted to collect his money, the constabulary were able to put all the pieces together. The shooter's identity was confirmed by Molly Melrose, a ten-year-old Girl Guide, who was selling cookies in the park that day.

ENDGAME: As Comedy
Chapter 49

The young clerk inside the Type bookstore on Queen Street West, in the city known as Toronto the Good, is leaning on his broom, looking out the window. It's closing time, he has been sweeping up after a busy day in the shop. He sees a man sitting on the bench across the street under the old oak tree. The man is alone and appears to be talking to himself.

"Poor guy," thinks the clerk. "Probably from the hospital up the street. Odd looking dude. Wonder where he got those knee sox. Probably has everything he owns in that old burlap bag."

As the bookstore clerk returns to his clean-up duties, the man he had been observing rises from the bench and stands looking across the street. He appears to be talking to the empty bench and gesturing in the direction of the bookstore. Then picking up the burlap bag from the bench and hoisting it over his shoulder, he walks through the fallen leaves, across the grass and the gravel to the street where he waits for the right moment, then dodging cars on both sides of busy Queen Street West, crosses cautiously and walks up to the front door of the bookstore. There he pauses to admire the stately pyramid of books in the bookstore window. His name is on those books. They are his books, *The Return of The Secret Viking*, piled high and handsome, beside an invitation to "Join the Book Launch." He opens the door and enters.

The startled clerk, still performing his day-end clean-up activities, responds to the stranger's entry with a quick, "Oh, I'm sorry, sir. We're closed."

"The door isn't locked, the lights are on, and there's a poster in your window inviting one and all to a book launch tonight. That doesn't sound closed to me."

"My mistake. Actually, two mistakes. I forgot to lock the door and I forgot to take the poster down."

"Why would you do that? It's a fine poster. You must be joking."

"Joking? Me? No. No, I'm not… uhm, not intentionally, sir."

"You don't recognize me, do you?"

"I guess not. Who exactly are you?"

"I'm Thorsten. That must ring a bell."

"Only faintly."

"How about Thorsten the Rood?"

"Wait a minute. The Viking warrior poet?"

"The very same."

"Go on. The Secret Viking? Truly?"

"That's the one."

"I can't believe it," says the clerk excitedly. "The 1300-year-old Secret Viking? Honestly?"

"Yes. Absolutely. In person. And for a limited time only."

"Oh, my! It's really you. This is a very special occasion."

"I didn't want to make too much of it, but that's what I've been trying to tell you."

"How exciting! There must be a reason. To what do we owe your visit?"

"The book launch. I'm here for the book launch."

"The book launch?"

"The book launch of *Return of The Secret Viking*."

"Then I have some not very good news for you, I'm afraid."

"Go ahead. Hit me with it."

"The book launch was yesterday."

"Yesterday? Are you saying I've missed it?"

"I'm afraid so, sir."

"I don't believe it."

"I'm sorry… I'm very sorry about that, sir. I don't control the timetable. I'm just a clerk."

"Bloody Hell! How embarrassing. I'll just slip out quietly then. Don't let on I was here."

ENDGAME: Old Tricks
Chapter 50

"I see you're up to your old tricks again, Thorsten."

"Old tricks? You're always putting me down, August. Have you never realized that? What tricks are you talking about this time?"

"Endings. Let's start with endings. First there are none. Then there are enough to fill a library."

"Oh, stop! Two endings are hardly a library. I've been known to do better."

"It's actually three, if you include this one."

"Alright, alright. You're saying we are now oversupplied with endings. So how are we to end this excess of endings? Take this ending, for example, the one we're in the middle of now. This ending, after all, despite being literally after all, may not be the final end. It may not even be the semi-final end. If it's neither of those ends, maybe it's the beginning of the end. All things, including endings, have beginnings. But I think it comes down to this, sometimes a book simply does not want to come to an end. It simply does not want to cooperate. It wants to go on and on. The novel, in a word, make that two hyphenated words, the novel is a non-stop motor-mouth. The book not only has a mind of its own, but it also has a mouth of its own and sometimes it just won't shut up."

"Does this mean you are no longer 'morbidly uncomfortable' with the concept of endings in general?"

"That hasn't changed. Let me point out that even with this cascade of endings, none of them ends for sure. True, the endings are many, but they are not permanent. These are unending endings because the author is not the one in control. The book is a stubborn monster. It always wants its own way. Or maybe it thinks it's Gee Oh Dee and yearns for its own parade."

"You once noted that Gee Oh Dee didn't have a parade..."

"No, but have you forgotten? Santa Claus does. And we all know what his job is. As the end draws nigh, the book always has one more gift to offer. It wants to bring you one more thought, tell you one more thing, share one more idea No matter what, there always seems to be more book, more story, more tale to tell, more secrets to share, and more surprises, and also a sequel and then a sequel to the sequel, all knocking on the door, coming up the walk, or driveway, or on an elevator, plus anything the author can dream up and dredge up and write up in order to stall, to delay, to avoid calling it quits, so as not to commit to finality but to scratch away and scribble on."

"And never say die?"

"Well, it's worked so far."

MARTIN MYERS

Martin Myers is the author of six comically philosophical novels: The Assignment, Frigate, Izzy Manheim's Reunion, The Secret Viking, The NeverMind of Brian Hildebrand, and the Return of the Secret Viking. He is also the author of a non-fiction work, The Urban Loft, a sort of renovator in the wry memoir masquerading as an architectural coffee table book.

His fiction has won wide praise in the media and in literary publications in Canada, the US, and the UK. The popular press compares Myers' work to that of Mel Brooks, Woody Allen, Monty Python, and the Marx Brothers while one literary critic ranks it with "Joyce, Barthelme, Nabokov and Borges for scathing inventiveness that makes readers laugh out loud and then in an afterthought of conscience, question their own ethics, morals and reality." If pressed to define his style, Myers describes it as metaphysical mystery.

His career has been a chequered one comprising such diverse vocations as broadcaster, magazine editor, actor, publisher, puppeteer, comic, TV time salesman, copywriter, restaurateur, car wash operator, realtor, broker, professor and novelist, among others. He graduated from the University of Toronto and post graduated from The Johns Hopkins University, Baltimore, Maryland. For two years, he was a Visiting Associate Professor at the University of Toronto and taught as well for five years in writing workshops at the U of T and York University, where he claims to have learned more than his students.

On March 28, 2024, the author of this book , Martin Myers, died. He did not live to see this book published and in print. We have faithfully followed his every wish and produced a book of which he would be proud.